DARK TRADE

A gripping crime thriller full of twists

HELEN H. DURRANT

Published 2017 by Joffe Books, London.

www.joffebooks.com

© Helen H. Durrant

ISBN- 978-1-912106-60-8

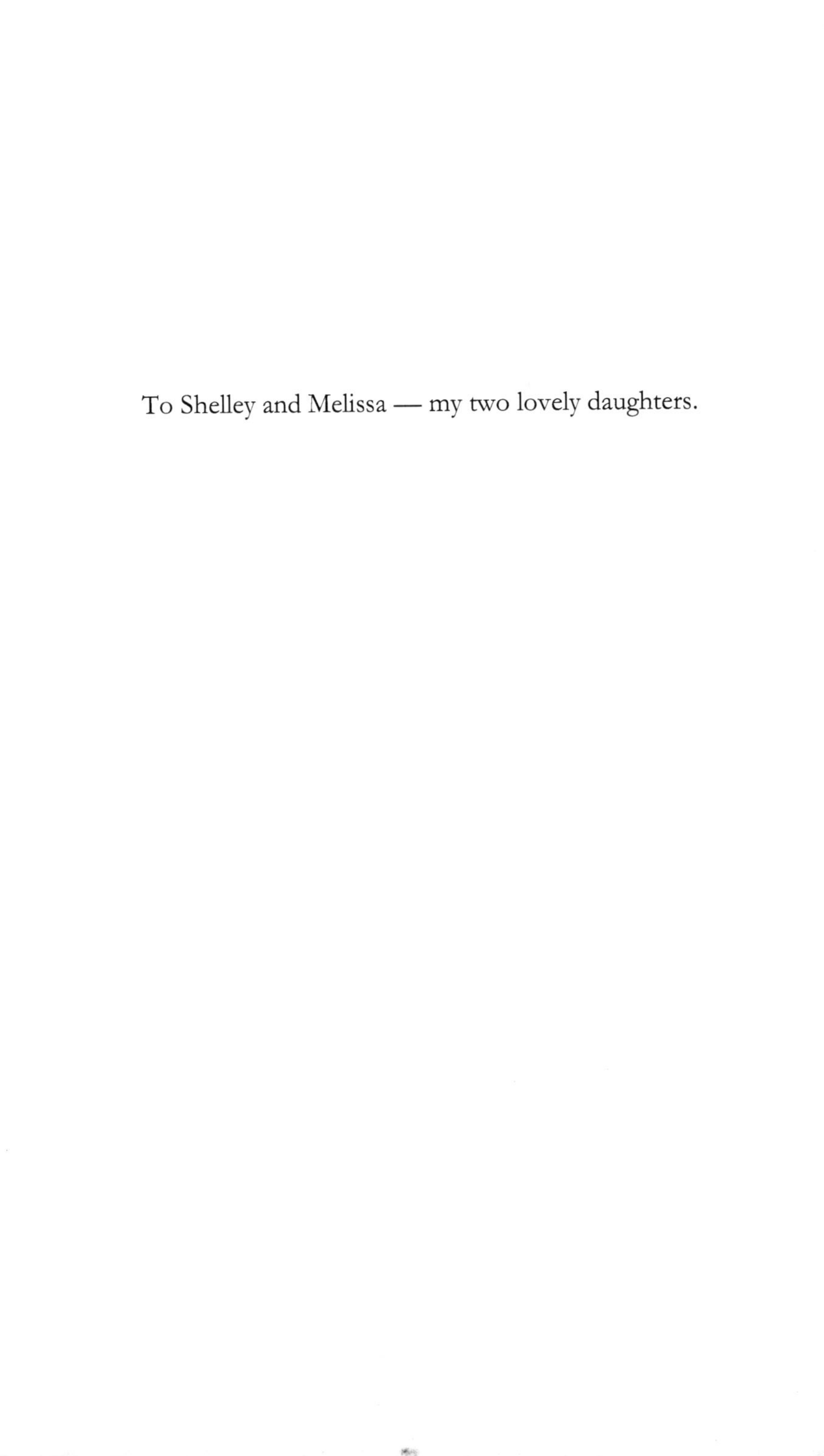

To Shelley and Melissa — my two lovely daughters.

Prologue

The knife slid in between the ribs, the tip positioned at the fifth intercostal space, then six inches of hard steel driven upwards. A split second later it entered his heart.

"Sorry. Nothing personal."

The kid turned, squinting up at his assailant. A strange face, smiling down at him, followed by a sharp pain as the knife was yanked free. For a moment he was stunned, frozen as his brain tried to process what had happened. His hands and eyes flew to his chest. There was blood, more than he'd ever seen. He sank to his knees, unable to scream. Shock and disbelief had taken away his voice. Seconds later he was dead.

* * *

Pocketing the knife, his assailant bent down and kicked him onto his back. He straightened the boy's legs, and neatly folded his arms across his chest. He put a hand to the jacket pocket — nothing but a few coins. No wallet, mobile or anything else to identify him. Made the job easy, just as Mickey liked it.

"A practised hand, I'd no idea. Boss'll be impressed," the driver said as Mickey slid into the passenger seat.

"He's not my boss. I work for myself. Just get me out of this poxy car park."

"Don't get shirty with me."

The killer examined the meagre haul. "He didn't have much. Only a kid. What did he do to deserve that?"

"Became a liability. Slicer likes things neat and tidy." The driver laughed.

"Slicer is an arse."

The driver looked at him. "Don't let him hear you say that."

"Slicer doesn't frighten me."

"Well, he should."

"Slicer can go to hell! You got my money?"

"Slicer said when it's over."

"He's dead. It's over. You don't leave this car until I get paid." There was menace in the words and the driver gripped the wheel, looking ahead.

"He wants to talk," he admitted. "Pay you himself. Offer you a deal."

Mickey shuffled uneasily on the seat. "I don't do meetings. Ring him. Get me my money."

"Ring him yourself!"

Mickey didn't like this, it wasn't how these things worked. A name, a place and payment on results. Anything else was a complication.

"Where does he want to meet?"

The driver smiled. "That's better. Now relax. He's got a deal you will be interested in."

"Where?"

"I'll pick you up, same place, midday tomorrow," said the driver. "Don't worry. Slicer will have your money."

"He better have."

"Cocky bastard, aren't you, kid?"

"No. What I am, is good."

Chapter 1

Day 1

Another look in the mirror. A tweak of his tie. Steel grey — a perfect match for both his shirt and his mood. Stephen Greco closed his eyes, and a weary sigh escaped his mouth. What was he doing?

"You look smart." The voice behind him was reassuring, and there was a comforting hand on his arm.

"Thanks, Pat."

The woman smiled at his reflection. "Don't be nervous. You'll be great. This is what you've always wanted — promotion to DCI. Remember?"

He gave a half-hearted smile. "That was before . . ." He averted his eyes from hers. His stomach tormented him whenever he spoke of Suzy. "Now I'm not so sure."

"You need to work, Stephen. It's good for you. Suzy wouldn't want you moping. She'd want you to get on with your life. And Matilda needs you to be on top form."

Mention of his young daughter put the smile back on his face. Pat was right. Life hadn't been up to much for his six-year-old daughter recently. She asked about her mother constantly — when she was coming back. Greco had tried to explain, but he didn't have the words, and even if he had, he doubted the child would understand.

"Are you sure you want to do this, Auntie Pat? Once I get back into the thick of it there's no turning back. It's a big commitment. You've given up your independence to move here."

"I see it as a fresh start, for us both. Make no mistake, Stephen, I need this every bit as much as you do. You can't do the job if you're worrying about Matilda all day long. And me," she smiled, "I was stagnating in that village."

He grimaced. "You're right, as usual. But make no mistake, you've got the rough end of the deal. A dysfunctional depressive and a small child to look after."

"I'm only too pleased to have a purpose again. I was going to seed. Looking after you and the little one will keep me sane." She smiled at him.

"I don't know about that. Matilda can run rings around the both of us. What's more likely, is that she'll wear you out."

She whacked him with a tea towel. "I'm fifty-eight! There's plenty of pep in me yet."

Now for the ritual. Greco hated the way he was. But since his wife Suzy's death, his OCD had become worse. He checked his reflection one more time, swept the blond hair from his forehead. He clapped the right pocket of his suit jacket. His mobile was in place. Retrieving it, he looked at the screen. Plenty of battery. Next, he picked up his wallet and badge from the sideboard. Finally, a short walk across the sitting room to the photo of Suzy, the one that stood in pride of place on the mantelpiece. Lifting it tenderly, he traced the outline of her face with his finger, then kissed it. All was in order. Time to go.

Pat called through from the hallway. "Visitor, Stephen! It's McCabe."

Greco pulled a face. What now? He could hear Pat at the front door. A short conversation and bursts of laughter. Moments later she reappeared with Detective Superintendent Gordon McCabe in tow.

He came straight to the point. "Morning, Stephen. We've got a dead 'un on Gorton Road multistorey. The call's just come in, so I thought you and me would take a look."

"Murder?"

"I'm afraid so. Pathologist's taken a quick look and reckons that whoever put the poor kid out of his misery was no amateur. It looks like the Knifeman has struck again." He grimaced.

"That makes two. He's getting a taste for it."

"No, Stephen, what he's doing is getting away with it. Same method both times. Victim killed, laid out, and left without any useful evidence."

"*Knifeman?*"

"Nickname the team gave him because of how the victims are despatched. This one knows what he's doing alright. One stroke, bypassing the ribs and straight into the heart. That takes skill."

"Got time for a mug of tea, Superintendent?" asked Pat.

"Sorry, love. We've got to dash."

Greco saw McCabe taking in his aunt, his eyes sweeping over her form. He looked impressed. Pat Greco was an attractive woman, and his new boss had a reputation.

"We'll visit the scene together. I'll leave you and your team to find out who he was. Won't be easy. He's young, Asian-looking, and his clothes have seen better days. He could have been living rough. Uniform did a cursory search, but found nothing on him. Stinks of something nasty, Stephen. He looks like a drug runner, and so did the other kid. These killings look like executions to me."

"Executions. You're thinking gang or drug related?"

"It's a possibility we can't ignore. If the dead kid was carrying drugs, the lab will tell us."

"We had gang problems in Oldston," Greco told him as they made their way to the waiting car.

"This is a very different ballgame, lad. It's not a few small operators hanging around some rundown estate. This is city-wide organised crime. Drug importation, prostitution, people trafficking. There are several minor villains who run things locally, but the big player in Manchester is Vincent Costello. All the local dealers get their stuff from him, and he takes a generous cut. He might live out in deepest Yorkshire but he maintains an iron grip on his operation here. Trouble is, proving it."

"This could be an attempted takeover?"

"God help us if it is. We'll be picking up bodies off every street corner."

Greco hadn't known him for long, but he was warming to Gordon McCabe. He was a 'no frills,' get-the-job-done type, who spoke his mind. Born and bred in Manchester, he had no edge to him. Superintendent he might be, but he had earned the position through sheer hard work. No graduate entry for him — he'd started out as a uniformed constable. But how long he'd stay in the job was anybody's guess. He wasn't a fit man. Overweight, with a face Greco could only describe as 'lived in,' he'd smoked all his life and was often breathless when climbing stairs. Greco didn't know exactly how old the superintendent was, but he had to be in his late fifties at least.

"D'you know this part of the city?" McCabe asked as the car pulled up on Gorton Road.

"No, sir. I'm still finding my way around."

"Most of the terraced streets round here were torn down in the fifties and sixties. The families were rehoused in them buggers." He nodded at the high-rise flats. "Modern housing was what was promised. A breeding ground for villains is what we got."

"But there is some nice property here. Those over there for example, sir." Greco looked at the modern low-rise blocks and new houses that spread out from the main road into the backstreets.

"Aye, those new 'uns might be alright. But there's still a lot of poverty here. Old stuff that should be condemned — and them eyesores. That's the Lansdowne Estate." He gave another nod at the tall blocks. "Not a place to wander round on your own at night."

The body was lying on the second level of the car park. A young olive-skinned, dark-haired male, flat on his back. His eyes were open, staring up at nothing. His clothing was dirty and worn. His legs were stretched out together in front of him and his arms were neatly folded across his chest. Obviously the killer had had plenty of time.

Greco was looking around. "Why wasn't he found earlier? This is a busy car park."

"Cheeky buggers taped off this level. Chap on the gate came up here early doors to investigate and found him."

The pathologist at the scene was Bob Bowers, who greeted him with a smile. "DCI Greco. Congratulations! I heard about your promotion. Mind you, it's a double-edged sword. All it gets you is more responsibility, and you've still got all this stuff to sort out."

"Anything that'll help?"

"No ID, but I might find something when I get him back. Teeth are well looked after, so dental records might give us a name in time. I plan to do the PM back at the Duggan, this afternoon at about two."

Chapter 2

"Some of you already know DCI Greco. The rest of you met him in the pub last week," McCabe told the team. "So don't be shy. Give him your support. My gut tells me we're in for a bumpy ride with this one." He nodded at the incident board. "Introductions over. I'll leave you lot to get on with it. The chief constable wants me for lunch." He winked.

Greco had swapped Oldston station for the new headquarters of the Serious Crime Squad, on the outskirts of Manchester. The old police station that had served Openshaw had been given a makeover, and was now state of the art. The new office was streamlined, with huge windows that let in plenty of natural light. Greco had his own space behind a frosted glass partition. His office furniture was new, and his desk sported a brand new laptop.

Some of the old team had come with him at his request — DS Jed Quickenden, aka *Speedy*, and DC Grace Harper. Grace was both a colleague and a friend. During the worst of times, Greco had been able to lean on her, and he valued her support. Of all his old team, she was the one he'd been closest to. This was something Grace sometimes misinterpreted.

Until a week ago, he'd had no idea who else would be joining them. The new members of the team were a DI, Leah Wells, and a DC, Joel Hough. Apart from half an hour spent in the pub, where he learned that both had transferred from Manchester Central, he knew little about them.

Leah Wells was his age. She was a tall, lithe woman, who looked as if she was often at the gym. Long dark hair tumbled untidily across her shoulders, and her eyes were blue. Cornflower blue, he'd noticed, the same shade as his daughter's. She had a wide smile and a slightly turned up nose. Leah Wells was pretty. The only drawback was that her clothes were too casual for Greco's liking. Today she was in a pair of well-worn faded jeans.

Joel Hough was young, in his early twenties. He was tall, dark-haired, with heavy glasses which made him look geeky. His speciality was IT. He sat at his desk, staring at his computer screen. He didn't even look up when Greco addressed the team.

"Unknown male, still in his teens I'd say. Stabbed, and his body laid out on the floor of the multistorey car park on Gorton Road," he began. "There was nothing on him to help with identification. No mobile either. I doubt this was robbery. The kid didn't look as if he had two halfpennies to rub together."

"Perhaps the killer was disturbed," Grace offered.

"I don't think so. The killer laid him flat on his back, straightened him out, and folded his arms, which takes time. We don't know if anything was taken from the scene. But he could have been running drugs. Bear that in mind. I've read the file on the individual called 'the Knifeman.' McCabe reckons this has all the same hallmarks, and I agree with him."

"Current thinking is that he is a specialist hitman," said Leah Wells.

"The two killings have been young men. We suspect the first was delivering drugs around the Lansdowne Estate. It is possible that the second one was too."

"If that's so, then they'll be local, known. The multistorey is only a stone's throw away from the Lansdowne," Grace said.

Greco nodded. "That could be right. Our latest victim is young. Someone should miss him before long, and call it in."

"If we are going with the killings being drug related, we have to consider why they are different from the norm," Leah pointed out. "The usual way of disposing of a rival is with a bullet. Quick and simple. I'd like to know what's changed."

"Bullets get attention, media and the like," Greco reminded them. "The headlines after that doorstep shooting in Beswick last year went on for weeks. The Knifeman is a shadow. No one sees, no one hears. That makes the incidents less newsworthy. The doorstep shooting got the media attention it did because there was a screaming match first, and a group of kids were playing in the front garden."

"I haven't heard anything on the streets about a bust-up in the drug gangs, or a new face on the block," one of the PCs added. "If something was going on, there would be whispers all over. There's plenty of dealing, but it is strictly controlled. Each firm has its own territory."

"I've checked the HOLMES database, sir," Joel Hough piped up, his face turning red as all eyes turned his way. "It fits no other method of killing in our area. Stabbing features widely, as you'd expect. But not the skill, or the way the body was left."

Speedy nodded. "In that case, he's a new operator. What we have to find out, is who he's working for."

Greco pointed to the photo of the victim on the incident board. "For now, we'll concentrate on finding out more about him. We need a name. We need his life up there before we make any assumptions. He'll have family. They need to know what's happened, fast." He looked at Grace. "Check missing persons. Go back a while. If he was living rough, the call will not have come in recently. Any males reported in the last few months, put them on the board."

"That road is covered by CCTV," Speedy offered. "Although not the entrance to the multistorey. Inside, the coverage is patchy. On the floor we're interested in — nothing."

"You get on it. We've no idea what we're looking for, but at least we have his photo. Someone might recognise him. DI Wells and I will attend the post mortem."

She smiled. "Bit formal that, sir. Call me Leah."

"Want me to put these files in your office, sir?" Grace interrupted.

"I'll take them, Grace." Greco had noticed the wary look Grace Harper gave Leah. He was well aware that Grace had a soft spot for him, but the problem was, all he wanted was to be left alone. He liked Grace. She was young, attractive, and, like him, she loved her job. But for now that was as far as it went.

PC Gareth Dobbs was putting down the office phone. "We've had a report of an altercation last night, outside the multistorey. A heated argument between two blokes. The man who rang it in heard about the killing on the local news and wondered if it was relevant."

"It might be. There again, how many arguments are there along that stretch of road? It leads straight onto the Lansdowne," said Leah.

Greco shrugged. "We have nothing else. We can't ignore this."

"He lives at 5 Sutton Close," the young PC told them.

"Leah, you and I will check out what the man has to say, then go to the Duggan." Speedy looked put out. Usually it would be him at the DCI's side. But Greco needed to get to know Leah Wells quickly, and he couldn't do that if he left her in the office staring at a computer all day. He looked around the room. "Anything else comes in, let me know immediately."

It looked as if McCabe was right. They were in for a bumpy ride, and not just with the case. He'd seen the looks. Speedy and Grace were finding the transition difficult.

"Want me to drive, sir? I know the area," Leah offered.

Greco nodded, and they made their way down to the car park. "Tell me about the gang setup around here."

"Vincent Costello is the top dog. Has been for decades. The problem we have is making anything stick. All the gangs pay him to leave them alone, and they wouldn't dare cross him. From time to time we'll nail one of them. When that happens, Costello's mob drops the poor unfortunate like a hot brick. There are a couple of prime movers. There's one in particular who takes care of things in East Manchester."

"Ray Shaw."

"Yes, or *Slicer* Shaw as he's known on the streets. He's tough. He earned his nickname because of what he's done to the poor sods who've crossed him or Costello. Not that we can prove anything," she added. "On the surface Shaw comes across as a successful businessman. He owns a club in the city. It's very popular, attracts a lot of wealthy people. But don't be taken in, he's as dodgy as they come."

"McCabe gave me a file on him."

"No need to tell you the gory details then."

"You're local. Is that how you know so much about Costello?"

"I've done my homework. Costello's main home is in Yorkshire. Last year I worked with the team over there who were trying to get him on a murder charge."

"You didn't make it stick?"

"No, his legal team ran a horse and cart through every piece of evidence we had. In the end one of Costello's people took the rap. Poor bastard must have been in fear of his life to be willing to go down for murder."

"Are there any contenders in the frame for the post of rival?"

"It's difficult to know. I've heard nothing on the streets. I have a couple of snouts who give me good info. Word is, all's quiet."

Not that quiet. They had two bodies.

* * *

They pulled up on Sutton Close, a row of townhouses just off the main road. "We're only a couple of hundred yards away from the site of the latest killing, sir," Leah told Greco.

The area was heavily built up and overshadowed by the Lansdowne.

"You police?" The man who answered the door spoke in a gruff voice. "Proper police?"

"DCI Greco, and this is DI Wells."

"In that case, come in."

They followed him inside. "Like I told the bloke on the phone, it might be nothing, but you never know. I don't sleep much so I went for a walk last night. Can't say what the time was exactly, but it were late on. There were two of them outside the multistorey. Felt sorry for one of them, skinny lad he were, stood no chance against that bully."

Leah smiled at him. "Tell us what happened, Mr Barton."

"He were a young lad, foreign-looking. He looked as if he were waiting for someone. Then this big bloke pulled up in a car and started shouting at him. A few seconds later he got out, and pushed the lad around. I was only a few yards away. The lad told him to get lost but the bloke was shouting his head off. I shouted back at him. Told him to stop." Stanley Barton paused. "It were dark, but there's a streetlight there. He looked me full in the face. I recognised him. Told him so, an all. It were then he hopped back in his car sharpish, and drove off."

"Who was it?" asked Greco.

"Him from the paper — the *Chronicle*. That Tony Rouse. Pokes his big nose in everywhere, that one. I heard about stabbing on the news this morning. Might have nowt to do with it, but you can't afford to miss anything, can you?"

"Thank you, Mr Barton. I'll get one of the uniformed officers to take a full statement." Greco thought for a moment. "Did you hear any of their conversation?"

"No. Lad had an accent. Couldn't understand him. Rouse was talking about money though. At one point he grabbed the lad's arm and tried to pull him into his car."

"But he got away?"

"He pulled free and disappeared into the car park. He were slow, mind you. Lad were limping, as if he'd hurt his leg."

"Thanks, Mr Barton." Leah smiled at him again.

Outside, Leah said, "We should speak to this Tony Rouse straight away."

Chapter 3

Mickey had tried to be good. He'd got himself a decent job, even promotion. Worn a smart suit to work. Played the game. But underneath, the real Mickey still lurked. A person could not deny who they were at ground level. The real Mickey was bad, and he hated it. But Mickey also had skill. That skill was dirty, but it would help him achieve a long-held ambition. And involvement with Slicer was key.

"You've done well. Here." Slicer Shaw held out a bundle of notes. "Take the cash. You've earned it."

Snatching the money from the villain's hands, Mickey spat out the words. "Don't go thinking I enjoy any of this. I do it 'cause I have to."

Slicer sneered. "Don't give me that twaddle. No one who kills like that doesn't enjoy it. You're good. I don't want to lose you. I'm willing to pay big money to keep you close."

"You can get hitmen off any street corner."

"Not like you I can't."

"I'm not reliable. I disappear for months on end. I get black moods. I don't like who I am." Mickey was almost pleading.

Slicer Shaw roared with laughter. "Too deep for me, that. Never did understand you educated types."

"You got that wrong," Mickey hissed.

Slicer pushed the hood back off Mickey's face, and looked taken aback. "Not what I expected. And you're young."

Mickey jumped back. "Get your hands off me!"

Slicer whistled. "Nervous type. I'll remember that in future."

Slicer was tall and stout, with a florid complexion. Too fond of booze and blow, Mickey had heard. He had a long nose and was losing his hair. It was tricky to pin an age on him. Somewhere round fifty seemed likely.

"You're handy with a blade yourself. You didn't get the nickname *Slicer* for no reason. So why use me?"

Slicer laughed again, and called out to his driver. "The kid's got balls!" He turned back to Mickey. "I don't do a clean job. I'm too fond of seeing folk suffer. I slit the buggers open." He swept a finger down from his neck to his navel. "I leave them hanging. Not what's needed for the work I'm in. I need someone who can get to the target, finish him and get out. Do the job in minutes. Not the long drawn-out stuff I favour." His mouth curled into an evil smile. "Ever watched a man's guts drop onto the floor? Seen the mess a person's insides make when they're ripped free? I once made some dickhead lick his own kidneys." He laughed again.

The man was insane. Mickey felt sick.

"Are you in or out, kid?"

Mickey wanted to punch his lights out and run. But this was Slicer Shaw. There was no place he could hide, and Mickey didn't have a death wish.

"Okay. But I don't need a minder in future." Mickey nodded at the driver.

"He stays. I like confirmation. I need to be certain that the job's been done right. I don't like complications. Take this." Slicer handed over a mobile phone. "It can't be traced, and I'll do the topping up. Be ready. I ring and I expect an instant response. I don't do waiting. And I don't do excuses. I give you a target, and the job gets done. No questions."

Mickey nodded. There was no choice. But every part of him screamed that this was a big mistake.

* * *

Greco was no stranger to the morgue at the Duggan. It was where he'd suffered the worst moment of his life. The last time he'd been here, it had been Suzy that the pathologist was working on. Just walking through the glass front doors brought it all back. His stomach churned. He took a deep breath. Attendance at post mortems was not optional.

Greco and Leah Wells stood on an elevated parapet overlooking the work area. They had a clear view of the trolley below them, with the body laid out on it. The internal organs had already been removed, and were sitting in various stainless steel bowls.

Bob Bowers began. "I'd put him at between sixteen and twenty. He's not Caucasian, could be Asian, then again he could be Syrian or Turkish. He's also thin, and very undernourished. However, his teeth are well cared for." They watched as the pathologist turned him over. "He has a number of cuts and bruises. I'd say they are several days old. There is a particularly large bruise on his right flank. Plus a deep cut to his right thigh which has still not healed. It should have been stitched. There would have been heavy blood loss." Bob Bowers looked up at them. "He may have been living rough."

It was worth considering. But if that was the case, what had made him a target for the killer?

"Something rather odd. He'd eaten less than an hour before death. Olives, cheese, and smoked salmon mostly, washed down with orange juice. Not what I expected to find."

"A bit posh for someone living rough." Leah turned to Greco and raised her eyebrows.

"Dr Bowers won't have made a mistake," he assured her.

"In that case, it sounds like he'd been to a buffet," Leah whispered.

"He's had his appendix removed. The scar is old. The op was several years ago. Plus he has odd feet."

"What do you mean, odd feet?" asked Greco.

"Just that. There is a difference in the size," Bowers replied.

"A whole shoe size, to be precise." Doctor Roxy Atkins entered the room. "Expensive shoes, and handmade. They definitely don't go with the clothes he was wearing. Can I make a suggestion?" She smiled up at them. "Nothing he had on was a particularly good fit. His jeans were too long, and the arms on that pullover are too short. They may have come from a charity shop. A desperate lad, in desperate times."

"Not the shoes though?"

"No, I'd say the shoes were made for him."

Expensive handmade shoes and good teeth. The lad may have lived rough, and died without a bean, but it looked as if his family had money.

Bob Bowers concluded his examination. "I'll let you have the toxicology results as soon as they're ready."

"Anything else on him?" Greco asked Roxy.

"Not that I've found yet. I'm looking at what his clothes might tell us. Fibres, pollens, you know the stuff. Might give a clue about where he'd been, what he'd been doing."

"How's Professor Batho?" Greco asked, his eyes on the floor, knees shaking. Julian Batho had recently lost his partner. Imogen Goode had been slaughtered by a madman. Greco and the solemn professor had a lot in common.

Roxy shook her head. "Julian is on leave. It's hit him very hard. He's not coping well."

"I know exactly how he feels." The memories threatened to overwhelm him, and Greco turned and walked out of the room. He had to get out. He needed air.

* * *

"Charity shops it is, then," Leah said when she joined him outside.

"It's a bit of a long shot. It's unlikely anyone will recall selling those exact items of clothing."

"If we have nothing else, I'll give it a go," she said.

"Sorry I left like that," he said, not hearing her words. Leah was putting her jacket on. It was leather, and she was wearing jeans. He knew it wasn't mandatory to dress smartly for work, but her style irritated him. Her shirt was a different shade from the denims. The clash of colours bothered him. His OCD was raising its ugly head.

Leah was watching him. "I know what happened. It's okay to talk about it. If you want to, that is."

"It's that place. It no longer feels impersonal, strictly to do with the job. What goes on in that room, on that table, it's far too real. And we drag people in there to identify their loved ones. I didn't have a clue . . . Well, I have now."

They walked towards the car in silence. Leah finally said, "The food in his stomach is interesting. Where do you get food like that around the multistorey?"

"You can check that out. Find out where we can get hold of Tony Rouse too."

"Back to the station, sir?"

"Yes, Leah."

* * *

DC Grace Harper pointed to the computer screen. "What's that?"

"Nothing much — a bus queue, I think."

"That bus, the number fifty-two, it goes past that car park on Gorton Road. Look at him!" She pointed to a figure on the screen. "Suspicious, or what?"

"You think our killer catches the bus? Get real," Speedy scoffed, checking his watch.

"You got somewhere to go?"

"I promised Michelle I'd meet her in the pub across the road, then take her to that new wine bar in the Northern Quarter. The one that's always on the telly."

"Trying to impress, eh?" she teased. "You must be smitten. What's she like?"

"Young, pretty and she's really into me." He grinned.

"Wants her head looking at."

"I took her to the horse racing in Chester last weekend. We stayed overnight in a posh hotel. She's great. I like her."

Grace ruffled his hair. "You're giving her the wrong impression. Probably thinks you've got money. What does she do?"

"Michelle works for Henshaw Bros. The warehouse off the bypass? They sell stationery wholesale. She works in accounts."

"Sounds boring."

"That's why she likes me. I'm a bit of excitement."

"You're a bit of rough, more like. Look at the state of you!" She flicked a finger at his tie. "This has got half your dinner down it."

"What d'you think of the new DI?" he asked, rubbing at his tie.

"I'm not sure yet. She's got her eye on Greco."

"I think you're wrong. She's keen, that's all it is, Grace. No woman in their right mind would chase after him right now. He had plenty of problems before, what with his OCD. But since Suzy died . . . God knows what state his head's in."

"He'll come round. But I'm right. She'll make a play for him before long."

Speedy grinned. "Might do him some good. In the meantime, we still have to cope with his moods, and the long face. He's like a storm cloud on legs. I keep expecting him to burst at any minute."

"He's getting there, Speedy. He needs more time, not Leah Wells whispering sweet nothings in his ear." She slapped his arm. "So don't you go encouraging her."

Speedy turned to Joel Hough. "What do you think, Joel? Any comment to make about our leader?"

Joel shook his head. "Not my place."

"Speak your mind, Joel. Silence gets you nowhere." Grace noticed him blush. "We don't bite. We're just trying to get to know you better."

He shrugged. "Not a lot to know. I prefer to just get on with the job."

"Do you live locally?" Speedy asked.

"Local enough, Bredbury," he replied.

"Got your own place?"

"No, not yet, can't afford it. I live with my mum."

Grace saw Speedy grin. Given half a chance he'd tease Joel mercilessly about that little titbit. Time to step in. "I practically live with my mum," she said. "Or rather her with me. It's a childcare thing."

Greco entered the office with Leah Wells behind him. He went straight to the incident board, where he began to write. "An interesting assortment of food in the dead man's stomach. Yet he was dressed in clothing probably got from a charity shop. It doesn't square with his last meal."

"There are several pubs nearby. Plus the Millstone restaurant," Grace told him. "I'll check if they had anything on."

"There's no way they'd let him in there, dressed like he was," Speedy told them. "It's been done up. Fancies itself upmarket these days. God knows why, given where it is."

Grace went off to her desk to use the phone. Leah Wells was behaving like his bloody shadow, constantly at Greco's back.

"I'll start with the charity shops. It'll have to be tomorrow. They'll be shut by now," Leah told the team.

A job she could do on her own, Grace hoped. A short conversation later and Grace had the information she needed. "Sir!" she called. "Looks like it could be the Millstone. They did an evening buffet for the Rashid Clinic yesterday. It's a private clinic in Chorlton."

Greco looked at Joel Hough. "Do we have anything on the place?"

"Nothing on the system, sir. Give me a moment, I'll look it up on the net." Greco waited, tapping his foot on the floor.

Joel soon found it. "Wealthy clients, lots of paid-for procedures and expensive plastic surgery. Perhaps they simply felt sorry for the lad and fed him."

"I don't think so," said Greco. "How did the youngster get in there for a start? We'll call it a day. Tomorrow, let's see if we can get a name on that board."

"I've rung the newspaper," Leah told them. "They say Rouse is out doing an interview."

Greco looked at Joel. "Get his address tomorrow. Then we'll pay Mr Rouse a visit."

Chapter 4

Speedy stretched his long arms. "I'm ready for a pint. Anyone want to join me?"

"A quick one," said Grace. "You, sir?"

Greco wanted to go straight home but he'd learned that it was important to socialise with the team. "Okay, but just one."

"Mind if I duck out?" Leah chipped in. "Perhaps another time."

Greco didn't miss the look of relief on Grace's face. He'd see how it went, but he might have to have a word. He couldn't afford any jealousy or ill-feeling in his team.

"I won't either," Joel added. His gaze was still fixed on the computer screen.

As they made for the stairs, Speedy was on his phone. "Michelle is joining us," he told them, a beaming smile on his face. "Thought you might like to meet her."

Greco couldn't recall Speedy being keen for them to meet any of his previous girlfriends. Perhaps this one was serious.

The Gorton Arms was directly across the road from the station. A relic from the Victorian era, it still sported the original green tiles on the walls. It was on a main bus route into Manchester, and was rough and ready. Any late trade came from the backstreets. At this time of day the clientele were folk on their way home from work locally.

The instant they walked through the door, a young woman jumped off a bar stool and grabbed Speedy's arm. Greco was aware of strong, cloying perfume and a heavily made-up face. A very short skirt and big hair completed the picture. She was young, no more than twenty. A little too young for Speedy, thought Greco.

"Got you one in, babe." She kissed him, and took his hand to drag him away.

"These are some of my work mates . . ." Speedy tried.

"Thought we'd go for that meal, then back to yours. My flatmate's got her fella round tonight."

He tried again. "This is Grace. And this is the big boss, DCI Greco. This is Michelle."

She smiled at Grace but regarded Greco with a puzzled look. "So what do I call you?" She tilted her head, hands on her hips.

Greco smiled at her. "Stephen."

For reasons Greco couldn't fathom, she burst out laughing. "Sorry, but you don't look like a Stephen." She downed her drink. "Need this. Had a shit day at work." Her eyes were back on Speedy. "Mr Henshaw himself was in and had a right strop. Books don't balance, so we all suffered. He's had the VAT man on the phone. Miss Dent this and Miss Dent that. I'm sick of the sound of my name and that man's voice. Not a happy office."

She had shoulder-length, thick blonde hair cut in layers, which made it look untidy. Michelle Dent was pretty enough but she was tall and too thin. A lot like Speedy, Greco thought, and smiled to himself. Her voice was loud and penetrating. When she laughed, the whole pub heard. She didn't appear at all interested in Speedy's colleagues. She sat close to him, playing with his curly hair.

"What sort of day did you have, babe?"

"You don't want to know."

"Anything scary? Safe to walk the streets, is it?"

"I'd be careful," he warned. "We've got a knifeman on the loose."

She gave a little scream. Greco threw Speedy a look. He shouldn't be discussing the current case in the pub.

"Got a body, have you?" she asked, snuggling even closer to him.

Grace moved a few yards away from the couple. Greco followed and she changed the subject to police work. "The Rashid Clinic? Want me to give it a visit tomorrow? Show them the picture of the lad?"

"There'll be a briefing in the morning. I'll decided then what aspect of the case each of the team will pursue. We're jumping the gun in thinking this has anything to do with the Millstone, or the Rashid Clinic."

She shrugged. "Sorry, didn't mean to sound pushy. You know how it is, the need to be doing something." She gave him a half-hearted smile. "Perhaps you'd rather it was DI Wells who went. I forget you're still finding your feet as a DCI."

"It's nothing like that," he assured her. "I'm quite happy with the role. I know what you and Speedy are capable of. You're good detectives. I just have to let Leah and young Joel get stuck in, get to know their strengths. It's essential that they integrate quickly."

"You like her, don't you?"

The question was unexpected. Grace's bluntness often threw him. He had a quick look around to make sure no one could hear them.

"Not in the way you mean. For a start, I haven't known her long enough."

Grace nodded knowingly. "Well, she likes you. A girl can tell, you know. And what does that mean — you haven't known her long enough? Are you saying that in time you might like her?"

Greco couldn't tell if she was teasing him or not. She certainly didn't look amused. "They're new. Both she and Joel need my attention. I have to rely on them, trust them to do the job. That means I have to get to know the pair of them quickly. I am not looking for anything more than that. What part of the case I allocate to Leah is down to what she's best suited to. Nothing else." Greco wasn't sure why he was justifying his actions to Grace. He didn't want her upset. But he didn't want her getting ideas about him as a prospective boyfriend either.

"Sorry, wrong end of the stick."

Grace was obviously uncomfortable. He'd said too much. "We haven't spoken much since . . . since Suzy." He tried a smile. "But it's not because I'm avoiding you. Me and the world are not a good fit right now. I'm not easy to be with."

Grace pulled a face and tightened her blonde ponytail. "I did wonder if it was me. For a while back then we got close. After that, you didn't come near. I decided you regretted it and were giving me a wide berth." She smiled at him. "After what happened, Stephen, I thought that you and me . . ."

This again. Grace liked him, she'd made no secret of it. Dealing with her wasn't easy, and that was down to his own confused feelings. "It's because of what happened," he said. "You are a friend, Grace. I worry that you might get the wrong impression, imagine that I'm looking for more, when I'm not."

The words were out, but were they the truth? Wasn't it more about a fear of commitment?

She frowned. "Well, that's me told. So what about the young and talented DI Wells? Are you saying you don't fancy her either?"

More of her bluntness. Greco sighed. "You shouldn't say stuff like that. I have a job to do, and so does she. I'm not interested in a relationship with any woman just now, Grace. It's too soon."

Another peal of laughter from the far corner, and Grace put her hands to her ears. "I've had enough. Speedy is welcome to her. I'm off home."

This had nothing to do with Speedy's new girlfriend. It was all down to him. Had he said too much? He didn't want to sour their relationship, Grace was a good friend.

He should go home as well, but his head was too full of the case. Greco said his goodbyes and made for the door. Once outside, he checked a map of the local area on his mobile. The Millstone wasn't far. A quick visit would only delay him by half an hour, tops. As he walked to his car, he rang Pat and told her.

"Gives me an excuse," she said, sounding relieved. "I've had Gordon McCabe on the phone. He asked me out to dinner. Now I can let him down gently." She laughed.

Another complication. The super was chasing his aunt.

The Millstone wasn't too far from the pub. Greco parked up and walked towards the impressive entrance. It looked as if it had been recently refurbished. It was now an upmarket restaurant, with a bar and a large function room.

It was busy when Greco arrived. He went straight to the bar and asked to speak to the manager. The waiter appeared reluctant to call him until Greco showed him his badge. Why so cagey, he wondered?

The manager was a man called Smith.

"I'm interested in an event held here yesterday for the Rashid Clinic," Greco began. He took a headshot of the dead man from his pocket. "Was this man among those attending?"

Smith took the photo and scrutinised it. "Doesn't look well, does he? There was over sixty people here. I was kept busy."

"It's important, so think a little harder."

"The place was crowded. I was organising the staff and seeing to the food. I do remember it was for the doctors and their prospective clients. But him? Doesn't look the type." He looked at the image again and shook his head. "No, I don't think so."

Greco frowned. This was wasting time. "Are you quite sure? This man was found murdered this morning, and we have reason to believe he was here yesterday."

Smith's face hardened. "I said no," he growled.

"For someone who was so busy, you're very sure."

"Like I said, he wasn't here."

"Before I leave, could I have a copy of the menu from the event?" asked Greco.

The man looked puzzled. "It was nothing special, just a buffet and some drinks."

"I'd still like an exact breakdown. If you don't mind, Mr Smith. Then I'll say goodnight."

Smith handed him a sheet of paper. "Here, it's our standard event fare. If you're looking for a troublemaker, try that hack from the *Chronicle*. He was here, uninvited, and upsetting people."

"Which particular *hack*, Mr Smith?"

"Tony Rouse."

<h1 style="text-align:center">Chapter 5</h1>

Day 2

"We need to speak to Tony Rouse," Greco told the team. "That reporter working for the *Chronicle*. He spoke to the victim outside the multistorey. I'd like to know what about."

"Why would someone like Rouse be interested in a homeless lad?"

"I've no idea, Grace. But it must have been important. I called in at the Millstone on my way home last night. Rouse had put in an appearance there too. It looks to me like he may have been following the lad."

"In that case, he's chasing a story, sir," Speedy said. "Did you find out if the victim was there?"

"The manager couldn't be sure. Grace and I will go and find Rouse this morning. Leah — you and Speedy go and speak to the Rashid Clinic. See if anyone who was present at the event can shed any light."

"The reporter angle could be a way to go, sir." Grace was smiling broadly. "We should let the press and media have the picture of the lad. It might jog someone's memory. Even better, it might attract the attention of a family member. It could save us a lot of legwork."

It was a good idea, and Greco nodded at Grace. "Joel, will you arrange that? Then it's back to the CCTV, I'm afraid."

"No probs, sir."

"Do we have an address for Rouse?"

Joel was busy on his computer. "The newspaper gave us the one they've got for him. But it says here the flat is rented out to his mother."

"Print out the address, Joel. We'll go and have a word. If he's not in, she may know where he's gone."

"Do we release the photo?" asked Joel.

"Okay, but just tell the press that we found the body with no ID. Not that he was murdered. Any other information is under wraps for the time being."

"The mother lives on the Lansdowne, sir." Joel passed him the address.

McCabe entered the office in time to hear his words. "The Lansdowne, eh? I'd wear a tin hat if I was you, Stephen. Any hint that you're police and we'll have to send in the armed squad."

"It can't be that bad, surely?"

"Put it this way, I've not been on that estate since I got this." McCabe held up his left hand. The tip of the little finger was missing. "Came at me with a bloody machete. Thought the bastard had taken my arm off at the time. Bled like a pig."

"We'll be careful."

McCabe nodded. "Just the two of you, and don't take a uniform. Don't want to invite trouble."

* * *

"It's a while since I was here. The estate is falling down," Grace said.

She was right. Greco hadn't seen such a depressing place in a long time. The Lansdowne Estate consisted of four tower blocks. None of them looked to be in good repair. The spaces between them were barren. Rubbish had collected by walls and in corners.

"No rubbish bins," Greco observed. "If there were some, folk might at least try to keep the area tidy."

Grace smirked. "Trust you to notice that. But you're wrong. They'd use them as drug drop-off points more likely. Look around. See how many young lads on bikes there are riding up and down the place? Drug runners, the lot of them, bet my life on it. A couple of years ago some loon left a hand grenade in one of those bins. It was just luck that no one was killed. Since then the council won't even consider replacing them."

"There are no houses, just the tower blocks. Not even a parade of shops."

"Used to be. There were two dozen or so houses over that way, but they were knocked down to make way for the tram lines. The shops were never a bright idea. One or more of them was broken into on a weekly basis."

"Where do the Rouses live?" asked Greco.

"Trojan House, that one there." Grace pointed. "Fortunately for us, the flat's on the second floor. What's the betting the lift's out."

The door leading into the tower block was hanging off its hinges. Inside, the concrete steps up to the higher floors were chipped and crumbling. The place was bleak and cold. Every sound echoed.

Climbing the staircase was a nightmare. Greco tried to avoid putting his hand on the rail. It was so dirty it was difficult to tell what colour it had been originally. Finally they reached the second floor deck. "What number?" he asked.

"Twenty-three." Grace knocked but got no response. "It doesn't look lived in." She tried peering through the window. "Rouse must make a bob or two. Fancy leaving his mum in a dump like this!"

Greco had to agree. The windows were filthy and a pile of leaves and rubbish had accumulated in the doorway. "Not many visitors, by the looks of it." He knocked again.

He and Grace were about to walk away when a voice called out from inside.

"We're looking for Mrs Rouse. Can you open the door?"

They heard movement inside the flat and the sound of a television. Suddenly the door was pulled open and an elderly woman looked out.

"Who did you say, love?"

"Mrs Rouse. We're the police." Greco showed her his badge.

"Can't see without my specs, love. You're not from the gas board, are you?"

"No, we're police," Greco replied patiently. The woman was thin with wispy grey hair. She looked in need of a square meal and some new clothes.

"Who are you looking for, love?"

"We're here about Tony Rouse, your son."

"He's not here. He's not been near in weeks. I don't know where he gets to."

"But he does still live here?" asked Grace.

"Now and then. He flits about. Last I heard he'd got himself one of those places in town, in a block of flats in Spinningfields. Said it was more convenient for work."

Grace smiled at her. "Does he visit?"

No answer to this. "Come in."

The front door led straight into the sitting room, which looked like a junkyard. It didn't appear as if anyone had done any cleaning or put the rubbish out in months. Greco shuddered. The place made his skin crawl. There was no way he could sit down.

"Have a seat. I'll get some tea."

"Please don't bother," Greco said hastily. "Do you have a phone number for him?"

"I do, if I can find it."

They watched as she moved some of her stuff about. Finally she rummaged in a handbag and passed them a slip of paper. "There. It's his mobile number."

Grace took it and copied it down. "Put it back safely, Mrs Rouse, in case you need it again."

"Is he in trouble? Chances his arm that one. Mixes with some right types. Tells me it's his job. But he'll get his head kicked in one of these days if he's not careful. Reckons he drinks with Ray Shaw." Mrs Rouse shuddered. "Dangerous job, working for the paper."

"Slicer Shaw. Know him well, does he?" Greco asked.

"They both grew up around here, so yes, I suppose he does."

"I'm sure he knows what he's doing, Mrs Rouse, I shouldn't worry. We just want a word, that's all," Grace said.

Outside, Greco inhaled deeply, trying to get rid of the stench of that flat.

Grace nudged him. "It's not her fault. She's old. She's got no one but Rouse. That son of hers obviously isn't up to much."

"His link to Slicer could be significant." Greco tapped Rouse's number into his phone. "Mr Rouse?" Greco nodded at Grace. "DCI Greco, East Manchester CID. I'd like to speak to you as soon as possible."

Greco listened. "The coffee shop on Gorton Road," he told Grace.

Chapter 6

A mobile rang. It was the one Slicer had given him. Mickey felt an instant jolt of adrenaline.

"Kid," began Slicer. "New mark for you. I'm texting you a name and a photo. Tonight, the Bull's Head. Posh place in Chorlton. Any time after eight."

He gave Mickey no chance to object. Slicer seemed to think the deal was done.

Mickey sat in front of his newly purchased, expensive laptop. A quick search and there he was, Slicer's mark. This one would give him no trouble. Middle-aged, soft-looking bloke in a suit. Doing stuff for Slicer was all very well, but Mickey was impatient. Once the rumours about the killings started, it was important for folk to add it up wrong, to see a turf war where none existed. Not yet anyway. What was needed was bad blood between Slicer Shaw and Costello. Mickey wanted the huge criminal organisation fractured at the core. Up for grabs.

Word on the street already had the two killings down to gang rivalry. Mickey would fan the flames. The blame must land firmly at Slicer's feet. Costello would think his old mate had been stirring it, planning to take the entire patch for himself. If Slicer disappeared, Costello would need a new right-hand man in these parts. Then Mickey would step in. It was a good start, but the plan needed some heat.

After Mickey had dealt with this mark, someone close to Slicer had to go. Someone who would leave the villain vulnerable. But not by the knife. That would put Mickey, aka 'knifeman,' squarely in the frame. Something different was required. Something the police would attribute to Costello. The force would spend months chasing their tails trying to stop a gang war. Slicer would assume Costello was coming after him next. Meanwhile, Mickey would move the plan up a notch.

What Mickey needed was a gun. For an execution, Costello-style. It would ensure that suspicion fell elsewhere. He knew someone who could supply what he needed, in one of the flats in Trojan House. Mickey had money now. Time to make a deal.

* * *

"She needs a visit from social services," Grace said once they were back in the car.

"I doubt she'll thank you for that. It's not our place to interfere." Greco shuddered. "That flat needs a damn good clean. How do people live like that?"

"I'll certainly be having a word with that son of hers. The poor woman needs help."

Greco nodded. "That's the place over there. Better keep your feelings under wraps, Grace. Keep the conversation with Rouse on track. We need him to talk to us. I can understand your concern, but we have a job to do."

"Come off it, Stephen. What sort of bloke leaves his elderly mother in a place like the Lansdowne, alone and fending for herself?"

"Unpalatable as it is, it's not our problem."

Greco parked the car in a side street and the two walked to the café. "Do you know what he looks like?" asked Greco.

"His smiling face stares out from the *Chronicle* most nights," Grace said. "He's not a very nice man. Tony Rouse likes to dish the dirt. Holds nothing back. If it's got a grubby underbelly, he'll be rooting around in it."

"I know you're angry, but don't antagonise him, Grace. We need information, not his newspaper blasting us for police harassment. Take a deep breath and let me do the talking."

The café was empty except for Rouse, who sat against the back wall, his face in his notebook. He was a big man, out of condition, middle-aged and losing his hair. He was wearing a suit that had seen better days.

He greeted the two detectives with an oily smile. "You'll be DCI Greco? How can I help?"

They sat down opposite him. "Last night you were seen talking to this young man at the entrance to the multistorey on Gorton Road." Greco showed him the photo of the victim. "Do you know him?"

Rouse studied the photo. "I did speak to him. Not that I got much back in return." He handed the photo back. "I've no idea who he was. Just a lad down on his luck. I gave him some small change for a sandwich. Why? Has he complained?" Another smile.

"You argued with him about money. You were heard."

"I gave him a couple of quid, he wanted more. There's no mystery."

His explanation sounded plausible enough.

"It was dark. There was no one about. The lad was edgy. To be honest, I thought he might try and mug me. Thought I'd bluster my way out of it." Rouse smiled again.

"Did you see where he went after you'd finished arguing?"

"No idea. I was glad to get away. I legged it to my car. Dodgy area that. Best avoided."

Greco frowned. "I think you were following him. We believe the lad had been to a restaurant called the Millstone. You were there too, before moving on to the multistorey."

"No law against eating out, is there?"

"Bit of a coincidence though."

"Look, copper. I don't know who he is, and I don't know what he was doing at the Millstone. I can't help you."

But Greco persisted. "In that case, tell us what you were doing there."

"The Millstone was holding an event for a clinic, the Rashid Clinic. I'm interested in knowing more about the place. It's early days in my research, but if I'm right in what I suspect, it's going to be a huge scoop. I went to the Millstone to try and talk to a couple of the surgeons."

"And did you?" asked Grace.

"No. Threw me out on my ear." He grinned. "You can't win 'em all."

"Tell us more about this scoop you're chasing, Mr Rouse," said Greco.

"I can't. It's all conjecture at the moment. But rest assured, the moment I get any sort of proof of what I suspect, you'll be the first to know."

Greco changed tack. "Did you see anyone else at the multistorey?"

"Some old bloke gave me a hard time for shouting."

That would be Stanley Barton.

"You're sure you didn't see anyone else, or where the lad went?" asked Greco.

"No idea. I had things to do. What is this? What's the lad done?"

"Gone and got himself murdered," Grace told him. "And you are one of the last people to have seen him alive, Mr Rouse."

Rouse held up his hands. "Not guilty. He was fine when I left him."

"Do you know his name?"

"Again — no idea."

"We have given his photo and details to the media. His image will be everywhere very soon." Greco saw the man's face drop. "Someone will come forward and give us a name."

"Wish you luck."

"You don't look happy with that, Mr Rouse. Worry you, does it?"

"Look, Miss—"

"DC Harper."

"I can't help. The lad was probably a drug runner off that damned estate."

"Is that why you spoke to him?" asked Greco. "Were you in the market for drugs?"

Rouse's eyes bulged and his cheeks puffed out. "Think what the bloody hell you like! But get off my back."

He got up and left.

"Doesn't like answering questions much. Slimy bugger, isn't he?" Grace said. "Where to now?"

"Back to the station. See what we've got between us when Leah and Speedy get back."

"D'you reckon he was telling the truth about the clinic?"

"If he was, it might explain things. He saw the lad leave, or worse, get thrown out of the Millstone and decided to speak to him."

"That could have been the argument Stanley Barton heard," Grace suggested. "Perhaps the lad wanted money for what he knew."

"We need a lot more information before we start concocting theories."

* * *

When they returned to the incident room, PC Gareth Dobbs and Joel were staring intently at Joel's computer.

"We've spotted something on the CCTV, sir," he told them. "See this figure on the road about a hundred yards or so outside the multistorey? Hood up, hands in pockets and keeping to the shadows." Joel took the film back so they could catch the figure walking along the pavement. "What d'you think?"

"It's not our victim — different clothes. He's tall and slightly built. Our lad was small."

"Keeps his head down. Looks nervous," Dobbs said. "He knows the camera is there."

"He's stopped. Looks like he's waiting for someone. He doesn't move for several minutes, then this." A car pulled up by the side of the road. "There's the figure again, and he's getting in."

"He gets into a car. He's driven a few yards, and then into the multistorey. So what was he doing? Getting a lift inside?" asked Grace.

Greco looked at them. "A meeting? Or the driver is making sure the job gets done properly. Always presuming that this is our killer, of course."

"That figure doesn't appear again, sir. So whoever he is, he went in and came out in a car."

"The film is time-stamped at eleven thirty. Can we get the number plate of that car?" Greco asked Joel.

"The image isn't very good, but I'll see what I can do with it."

"Send a copy to the Duggan as well," Greco said. "We need to know who was driving that car."

Chapter 7

Doctor Faisal Rashid was tall, immaculately dressed, good-looking but not in a startling way. He looked like a man you could put your faith in. He spoke reassuringly about procedures and treatments. He offered considerable expertise, but most of all he offered immediate treatment (unlike the NHS).

He'd poured his life into his vocation, and his business. Despite his talent, success hadn't come easy. The money to open the private hospital, the Rashid Clinic, had been hard come by. He worked long hours and had high standards. He expected the same from his staff, and most of all from his partner, Jason Horton. But lately Jason's interest had waned, which was a shame because the clinic was poised to take off in a big way. An expensive advertising campaign had borne fruit, and increasing numbers of wealthy clients were beating a path to their door. Jason was a brilliant cosmetic surgeon, who was affable and well-liked. But he had one big flaw. Jason Horton had a gambling problem.

Faisal Rashid's handsome face was pulled into a frown as he strode into his office, waving a sheet of paper at his PA, Sonia Jarvis. "When did you arrange this?"

"His wife rang this morning, Doctor. Doctor Horton spoke to her. Now Mrs Khan wants him transferred to Manchester General, under the care of Doctor Banister."

"He was having his treatment here. It was all arranged."

"Doctor Horton said there had been a setback. That perhaps it was time to look to the National Health . . ."

"Enough!" A nerve on Faisal's brow twitched with annoyance. "Doctor Horton is an idiot!"

Then his mobile beeped. It was yet another alert from the bank, the third this morning. He sat at his desk and tried to focus. He opened the lid on his laptop, and scrolled through his emails until he found the latest one from the hospital's account manager at the bank, sent within the last ten minutes. The clinic's account was overdrawn. This was the final straw. The balance had diminished consistently week by week over the past two months. Horton told him it was due to the increased cost of medical equipment. He was lying. Faisal had to put a stop to this before his world crumbled to nothing.

He slammed the laptop lid closed. With no money available and bills to pay, he'd be forced to take out a loan, something he'd avoided throughout his entire business career. Leaving Sonia cowering behind her desk, he went in search of Jason Horton. He found him coming out of the operating theatre, still gowned up.

"We need to talk. I don't understand what is going on inside here." Faisal tapped Jason's head. "You have drawn heavily on clinic funds. So much so that the account is now in the red."

"It's a mistake, Faisal. I'll sort it." Jason waved his hand airily. "There'll be cheques waiting to clear in the system. Don't stress so much, it's not good for you."

"How many more, Jason? When is it going to stop? You've used clinic money to fund your habit. If that isn't bad enough, the people you are dealing with are crooks. Carry on like this, drag us further into debt and this clinic will have to close!"

"You've got it wrong. It's like I said. I'll ring the bank myself and find out what's going on."

Faisal was not reassured. "Do it once you've cleaned up. I want the account put right today. Another thing, Khan can't transfer to Manchester. We are going to help him. You said you had it organised."

"You really do need to chill," Horton replied. "We've had a small problem. I'll ring him. Offer him alternative treatment. I'll persuade him to stay, trust me."

"You better had. We can't afford to have patients deserting. Him and the problem with the bank. You are becoming a liability." Faisal strode off. He needed to do the ward rounds. His patients were spending a great deal of money. They expected his attention, and he would make sure they got it.

* * *

Leah smiled at the receptionist sat behind the desk in the sumptuous waiting room of the Rashid Clinic. "DI Wells and DS Quickenden from East Manchester CID. We'd like to speak to one of the surgeons who attended the event at the Millstone yesterday."

"Certainly. Take a seat. Help yourselves to tea or coffee."

Speedy looked around. "Very nice. If I needed something sorting, this is the place to be." He grabbed a cup, filled it with hot coffee from a jug and sat down. "Wonder how much it costs to have work done here?"

"Depends what you're thinking of. Looking at you — nose job, ears pinning back. You could be worth a fortune in cosmetic procedures to this place." Leah laughed.

"Cheeky sod. If you weren't a DI and I knew you a little better, I'd get you for that."

"Don't mean anything by it. Just teasing. You must have something, despite the way you look. You attract women pretty easily."

"That wasn't just cheeky, it was damn rude." Speedy fashioned an arrow out of a leaflet and chucked it at her. He ran his long fingers through his curly hair. "What I lack in looks, is more than made up for by my charm and charisma. I like a good time, and so do the girls I date."

A man approached them. "Can I help? I'm Jason Horton, Doctor Rashid's partner. I was at the Millstone yesterday. It was my event. It was nothing big. As well as a few general surgical procedures we offer a wide range of cosmetic surgery. Since I left the NHS, that's been my speciality. The event was for potential clients. It's a very lucrative add-on to the business. A buffet, drinks, plenty of literature to read, and before you know it, the diary is full."

Jason Horton had scrubbed up and changed into a dark suit. Speedy put him at about forty. He was tall with classic good looks — a perfect advert for the clinic.

"Did you see this young man at your event?" Leah showed him the picture of their victim.

"I don't recall the face. And I would. Faces are my thing. Goes with the job." He smiled. "Plus, if you don't mind me saying, he doesn't look like our usual clientele."

"He wasn't," Speedy confirmed. "What about Tony Rouse? What was he after?"

Horton shook his head. "Again, I can't help you. I was talking to prospective clients for most of the evening. I wasn't clocking who was going in and out."

"The manager at the Millstone said Rouse was causing trouble. Didn't that disturb the party?" asked Leah.

"Not that I'm aware of."

Speedy knew Horton's type. Smooth, a practised liar. It oozed from every pore. "What did you eat?" The blank look on Horton's face annoyed him. "Surely you remember that!"

"A light buffet, smoked salmon as I recall. A selection of cheeses, and champagne."

"And olives," Speedy added. "You see, Doctor Horton, this young man was murdered last night. In his stomach we found exactly that — your buffet."

Horton looked puzzled. "So what are you saying? That I'm responsible for this young man's death?"

"No. We're simply trying to find out who he was," Leah told him. "We think Rouse was following him. So if we know what he was arguing about, it might help."

Horton shook his head. "Wish I could help, but I can't."

Leah smiled at him. "In that case, could I have a list of your guests? We have no choice now but to contact them all. One of them might recall the victim."

Horton looked horrified. Speedy was impressed. Leah had played a blinder. The last thing Horton wanted was the police on his prospective clients' backs.

"Rouse wants to run a story on us," he admitted finally. "He is convinced there is something dodgy going on in the world of plastic surgery." He laughed. "The man's mad. It's all nose jobs and facelifts. What does he think we're up to?"

"Did you ask him?" Leah asked.

"Wherever he got his information from, it's wrong. I told him so. I got annoyed and asked the doorman to throw him out. That's all there was to it." He looked at the picture. "As for him, I've never seen him before."

"You didn't answer the question, Doctor Horton," Leah prompted. "What does Rouse think you're up to?"

"He's a hothead. He muscled his way in, upsetting the staff. I'm afraid we never got round to discussing it. Can't be much anyway. We have an excellent reputation." He gave them a practised smile that didn't reach his eyes.

Chapter 8

Grace was studying the incident board. "Rouse was keeping something back. What do you think, sir? It could be he knows something about the Rashid Clinic. Should we get Joel to look at the place a bit closer? Check their accounts? See if Rouse is right. Make sure the doctors haven't been up to anything dodgy."

"It's a bit flimsy. We have no idea what Rouse has on them, if anything. I think he was spinning us a tale to put us off the scent. Going on about that clinic was a ploy to avoid talking about the victim. It's the lad we need to focus on."

"In that case, we should bring Rouse in. Perhaps a formal interview will loosen his tongue. Perhaps it was what you said, Rouse was looking to buy drugs and the boy couldn't oblige."

Greco wasn't sure. They needed more on the lad, his name, and where he'd come from. He caught a glimpse of the office clock. "We'll leave it until tomorrow now. It's getting on."

"Should get off myself. I tend to lean on my mum a bit too much where Holly is concerned. Not that Holly minds, she can wrap my mum around her little finger. You're lucky, having Pat living in. Bit like having a live-in nanny. Bet she's a good cook too."

"She is, but I don't think of Pat as a nanny. She's my aunt — my father's sister. She's always been someone I could trust."

"Wish I had a live-in somebody. Mum's great, but it would make life a lot simpler."

Greco was gathering his stuff together, getting ready to leave.

Grace stood watching him, arms folded. "Leah's a bit of a closed book. I haven't heard her make one comment about her private life. Odd, don't you think?"

"Not really," Greco replied. "She simply values her privacy. Can't say I blame her."

"Come off it, Stephen. Being in here is like living in a goldfish bowl. Things happen, as you well know. We all get involved, try to help, be there for each other. That's why it works so well."

"She'll talk when she's ready."

"Do you fancy going across the road for a drink? Kids will wait for another half an hour."

Greco was wondering what excuse to make when the phone rang. It was the desk downstairs.

"We've had a call, sir," the duty sergeant told him. "In response to the photo of that murdered lad you released. A young woman has been on. She gave me her number and asked if you'd ring her back."

"Did she say if she knew him?"

"Yes, she does. But she wouldn't say how or give her name. She left her number and asked if the investigating officer would ring her back. She was at work, and couldn't talk. She had an accent, sir."

This sounded like the break they needed. A name for the victim. More information from Rouse, and they might get somewhere. Greco shouted across to Grace as she made for the door. "We've had a response to the press release! A woman, not English. With any luck she'll know who he is."

Grace hung back, waiting, as he dialled the number.

A woman answered, speaking slowly, pronouncing every word with care.

"DCI Greco, East Manchester CID. You know who the young man is?"

"He is my brother," she replied simply.

Greco spoke softly. "I'm very sorry. It must have been a shock, seeing his photo plastered across the media like that."

"I have been worried about him for weeks."

"What was his name?"

"Jamal Ali."

"The photo wasn't very good. You're sure?"

"Yes. I can't speak now. We must meet. There are things about Jamal that you must know if you are to catch his killer. You will have to come here. I can't travel."

"No problem. Where are you?"

"I am in Brighton. I have work in a restaurant," she replied.

"Brighton!" Greco repeated.

"I'm sorry. It is a long way from where you are. But you must come. I can't get away. It is too dangerous for me. I think I'm being watched."

"Are you in danger?"

"I have friends here. They look after me." Nonetheless, she sounded nervous.

"What is your name?"

"Amani Ali. You will come tomorrow?"

Greco was thinking. It was very short notice, but she could have vital information. "Tomorrow, then. I'll ring you when I arrive."

"What was that all about?" asked Grace.

"A woman, Amani Ali. Says she's his sister." He wrote the name 'Jamal Ali' on the board under the photo.

"She gave me a name. She wants to talk to us urgently. Problem is, she's in Brighton."

Grace shook her head, then her expression brightened. "Nothing's ever simple, is it? But on the plus side, I like Brighton, it's fun. I've been a few times. Great for kids."

Ignoring her, Greco picked up the office phone and dialled McCabe. One quick update later and it was settled. McCabe wanted him to go, but not on his own.

Greco turned to Grace. "Seeing as how you know the place, do you want to come with me?" Her face lit up. "McCabe thinks she might say more to a woman, be more at ease. I can't take Leah, she's needed here to steer the case."

"So I'm second best?" Grace folded her arms and stared at him. "You're taking me because you have no choice?"

She said the words lightly, but Greco knew that's how she saw it. "It's not like that, Grace. It's work." He'd no idea what was going on in her head, but her attitude towards their relationship was bothering him more and more.

She smiled. "I'm only joking, Stephen. A short break in Brighton will do me good."

"It's not a holiday."

"We won't be working 24/7. There is always the night life, if we have to stay over." She winked at him.

"We will drive down and stay at least one night. Can you arrange things in time? I'm thinking of Holly and your mum." He wasn't going to be drawn into a discussion about how they'd spend any spare time.

"Mum'll be fine about it. But forget about that drink, I've got too much to do. Case to pack." She smiled.

"We'll take turns with the driving," said Greco. "I'll pick you up at six tomorrow morning."

* * *

Mickey ran his finger over the cold, hard metal. The bloke in Trojan House had come up with the goods. One Glock pistol, with silencer and a box of ammunition. The lot for a grand. The decision now — who to kill?

It had to be someone connected to Slicer. Someone close. Mickey hadn't been around the guy long enough to work out who his inner circle was. Certainly the driver, he was always at his back. The mark first. The driver would be there, making sure the job was done right. The driver it was, then. Keep things simple. Mickey would take him out on the estate once they got back. It would put suspicion elsewhere. Once Mickey started the whispers, the police would chalk it up to an escalation of the gang war. Slicer would blame Costello.

Mickey stashed the Glock in the inside pocket of his hoodie, and the blade in a pocket of his oversized combats. The meet was on Openshaw High Street. The driver would take them both to the pub car park in Chorlton. Once it was done, he'd drive them back.

It was a short walk across the estate, and out onto Gorton Road. Picking up the pace, he made it to the meet in a matter of minutes. He was in no mood for conversation. Slipping into the passenger seat, the killer sat silent and sullen.

The driver looked at him and chuckled. "What's this? You psyching yourself up? Is this how you get in the zone? The killing zone." He laughed. "Wish I could be so cool. I'm a bag of nerves before a hit. That's why I was so glad when Slicer found you."

Mickey hunkered down lower in his seat.

"Got no conversation, kid? Come on. It's a good fifteen minutes' drive to Chorlton. Entertain me."

"Get stuffed."

The driver laughed and turned the radio up loud. He spent the rest of the journey singing his head off to the music. Mickey was sick of the man. It would be a pleasure to get rid.

The driver pulled up a hundred yards from the pub. He'd told Mickey to go round to the back, as CCTV cameras covered the car park.

Mickey slunk forward, hood up, head down, keeping to the shadows. At the rear of the building, the kitchen door was wide open. Food was cooking in the large ovens. The smell was overpowering, the pans on the hob were making a lot of steam. A man was whistling somewhere inside.

Mickey made for the bar. It was crowded but the mark was easily picked out. He stood a few feet away, chatting to another bloke. Mickey ordered half a pint, and leaned against the wall, watching. This one was different. He was no druggie off the Lansdowne. He was well dressed for a start. Mickey could not imagine how someone like him would know a sleazebag like Slicer.

But the details didn't matter. Mickey smiled. This was easy money, another grand to add to the stash.

The mark was off in the direction of the toilets. There was nobody else about in the corridor. Mickey tailed him, the blade drawn and held close to his body. Inside the toilet, the mark turned to see who was at his back. Mickey struck. One movement, smooth and clean. A look of astonishment appeared on the man's face as he crashed to the floor. It had taken only seconds.

Mickey flipped him over onto his back and quickly searched his pockets. He removed a wallet, a mobile and a small notebook. After laying him out like the others, Mickey made a hasty retreat.

His only word to the driver was, "Done."

The driver started the engine, took a side road, and sped off back the way they'd come. "Neat work. You were gone ten minutes, tops. Slicer will be pleased."

"He was different from the other two."

"Someone needed a lesson in manners. That's all you need to know."

Mickey sat in silence. The driver hummed tunelessly to the radio. Not a minute too soon they were back on the Lansdowne.

"See you, kid." The driver grinned at him as he pulled up.

Mickey hopped out, and the driver moved off in the direction of one of the tower blocks. Time to make this happen. Slicer's work done, this one was personal.

The driver parked in the shadow of a tower block. Mickey was about fifty yards away. The driver got out of the car, threw a fag end onto the concrete and turned towards the main door. He was a big man, hefty and lumbering. Unlike Mickey, who had both speed and stealth. Within seconds, he had the driver an arm's length away from the muzzle of the Glock.

Mickey was high on excitement. He had not rehearsed this. It was seat of the pants time. He had one shot. No second chances. Eyes screwed up, breath on hold, he counted to three and pulled the trigger.

It was almost an anti-climax. There was hardly any noise, all Mickey heard was a throaty groan as the driver lurched for a second. He didn't even turn, simply fell forward onto the ground.

Chapter 9

Day 3

"It's not asking too much too soon, is it, Pat? I wouldn't go, but it is vital that we speak to this woman," Greco asked his aunt.

"It's part of your job. You have to do whatever it takes. Matilda and I will be fine, Stephen. You worry too much, you always did. Who is going with you?"

"DC Harper," he replied.

"Grace? She's nice. I like her. Matilda does too. She's asked if Grace's little girl Holly can come round after school one day soon."

"Grace is a colleague, Pat."

"She likes you. I've seen the looks."

"Imagination," he said, adjusting his tie.

"It's okay, you know. To want a relationship with someone else."

"It's too soon. Apart from which, I do not want a relationship with Grace."

"You're starting to wallow, Stephen, and it isn't good for you or Matilda. You need to reboot your life. Make a fresh start."

This again. "I thought I had. The job?"

"I'm talking about your private life. It would be good for you to take a woman out occasionally."

He sighed. "Like I said, too soon after Suzy."

"I don't like to say this, but you do remember that Suzy was about to leave you? That she was seeing someone else? It wasn't going to work. Plus you weren't married anymore when she died."

"And the bastard she was seeing murdered her." Greco banged his fist down on the sideboard. "He wheedled his way into her life because he had an agenda. Suzy was gullible, that's all it was."

"Wrong man, wrong choice, I agree. But the fact remains that Suzy was prepared to ditch you in favour of another man. If it hadn't been him, then it would have been someone else."

Greco felt sick. He'd gone over this many times in his mind. He wasn't ready to admit it yet, but he knew Pat was right.

"You can't spend the rest of your life mourning a woman who had fallen out of love with you."

He turned and faced her. "Pat! Please don't do this. A lecture is not what I need right now."

"Someone has to set you straight, Stephen. I'm the closest family you've got, apart from Matilda. So it's down to me." She took his arm. "Think about what I've said. Don't lose out on a good woman because of some fantasy in your head."

"I'm taking my bags out to the car." He grabbed the holdall, his laptop and a file of paperwork. His head was spinning. Pat was not trying to upset him, he knew that. Perhaps in time he'd be able to do as she wanted. But not right now. Suzy may not have loved him, but he had loved her. That wasn't a feeling he could ditch in a hurry.

He went back into the house. "I'll say goodbye to Tillyflop, then I'll have to leave. Want to hit the motorway before the traffic builds too much." He went up the stairs as quietly as he could and peered into his daughter's room. Matilda was still sleeping, her pink teddy held close. It was the last thing Suzy had bought for her. Since her death, the child hadn't let it out of her sight. He stroked the blonde hair from her face, and she stirred.

"Go back to sleep," he whispered and kissed her cheek. "Daddy will bring you back something nice."

* * *

"My mum is moving into mine until I get back." Grace said as they got going. "Makes life a lot easier. You sorted?"

"Would you ring in Amani Ali's mobile number, and ask Joel to get a list of calls. We need to know who she's contacted, and who has been ringing her."

"I see. That's how it is."

"Just do your job," he snapped.

"You look as if you're brewing for a punch-up, Greco. What's the matter?"

"I can do without the chat, if you don't mind. Driving is bad enough without having a verbal skirmish with you."

"Something's upset you. You're best talking about it. You know how you are. And try and remember, you're not the only one with problems."

Greco felt awful. He wasn't usually this bad-tempered, and rarely with Grace. Pat was one of the most level-headed people he knew. What she'd said to him had struck home. Suzy hadn't loved him. Not in the way he'd wanted her to. Well, he would have to face it. Pat was right. He needed to start again.

"I'm sorry. Bad mood. Pat gave me one of her pep talks before I left. It got me rattled, that's all. I shouldn't take it out on you."

"What did she say?"

Ordinarily he wouldn't discuss his feelings, or Suzy, with anyone. But he had spoken to Grace in the past, and she knew the score. "Pat reminded me that Suzy was more than happy to find someone else, and dump me. Told me that I was *wallowing* in self-pity. And that I need to get on with my life."

Grace chuckled. "Sensible woman. Got you banged to rights."

"Problem is, I don't know what to do about it. I'm a mess. I manage the job okay, but I stagger through my personal life."

"Try being less intense, Stephen. Chill a little. You might even have a go at enjoying yourself."

"Now you're making fun of me."

She looked at him. "No I'm not. You're young. Not bad-looking, for someone who so rarely cracks a smile. Give life a chance. That's all I'm saying."

"Thought I'd got it all boxed off. I'm buying the house we live in, the one Suzy was renting. Matilda is going to the local school. I'm trying to integrate, be normal, and keep things as they were for the child."

"And you'll get there. Want me to drive for a bit? Coffee at the next service station. Clear your head, and then I'll take over."

* * *

The traffic was kind, and they made Brighton in just over five hours. "Our hotel is on the front somewhere," Greco said, squinting into the sun.

"There is a lot of front, Stephen. What's the place called?"

"The Whitecliffe. It's somewhere near the pier."

"Great. Love Brighton pier. Me and my mum brought Holly about three years ago. We must have spent hours on there."

Greco pointed to a huge white Edwardian building. "That's it."

"It looks very grand. This is on expenses, isn't it?" Grace grinned. "Bet the rooms are lush. Can't wait to give the minibar a hammering."

"Don't push it, Grace."

The car park was at the rear. They parked up, grabbed their luggage and made for reception.

"I asked for adjacent rooms," Greco told Grace. "We'll have calls to make, work to do. It makes life easier."

"We're on the fifth floor." Grace nudged him, taking the key card from the receptionist. "The lift's over there."

"Busy place," Greco noted. There were plenty of people milling about. The hotel had several bars and a large sitting room for guests.

Grace smiled. "Coach parties. Look at the list of excursions on the board. Keeps the place going, I suppose."

But Greco was already on his mobile. "Amani Ali? DCI Greco, I've just arrived, whereabouts are you?" He stopped by a large ornate sideboard, and jotted down an address. "Okay, within the hour."

He turned to Grace. "You know Brighton? So you'll know where the Lanes are?"

"Is that where we're going?" There was a smile on her face. "Love it there. Lots of little specialist shops and cafes."

"We're here to work, Grace. This isn't some mid-week jolly."

"Come on then, whereabouts on the Lanes is she?"

"She works in an Italian restaurant. It's open till late. We can go and see her anytime. I have the address." He handed her the slip of paper.

"We can walk from here. It's only a few hundred yards over that way."

Chapter 10

DI Leah Wells stood poised beside the incident board. Present for the briefing were DS Jed Quickenden, DC Joel Hough and PC Gareth Dobbs.

"There were two more killings in the Manchester area last night, one of them on the Lansdowne. So that is definitely ours." She circled the word 'Lansdowne' on the board. "The other victim was found in the toilets of the Bull's Head pub in Chorlton. Not our area, I hear you say," she paused. "Nonetheless, despite what the South Manchester force will say, this one is ours too. The method was stabbing. The pathologist is certain it's the same killer that did for the two we're already investigating. One stroke, straight to the heart. There was no ID or mobile on the man, and he was laid out in the same way. However, we do know who he was." She wrote the name on the board, under the photo of the dead man. "Adam Crompton. That's all we have at the moment. We will interview his wife this morning."

"Interesting," Speedy said from the back of the room. "I wonder what he'd done to attract the attention of our knifeman?"

"We have no idea," she replied. "The killer will have been in the pub, waiting for his chance. He followed Crompton to the toilets and stabbed him there. We don't know how long he'd been hanging around the bar area. We need to speak to the other punters, ask if they recall seeing anyone watching Crompton. There is CCTV in the car park. Joel — get on it, please. Also the roads leading away from the pub. The estimated time of death was nine thirty. We will get his phone records too, and see who he's been in contact with."

"Let's hope the boss gets something on Jamal Ali," Speedy said. "Then we might stand a chance of piecing this together."

"I'm sure we'll get there, whether Greco's here or not," Leah snapped, and immediately regretted it. Two killings on her watch. They would be pushed. McCabe had spoken to her earlier. He was concerned about Leah's ability to handle the case in Greco's absence. Her promotion to DI was recent and this was the first big case she'd taken control of. Now she was taking it out on the team. Not what she'd intended. Leah Wells was only too aware of how much she needed them. But she was terrified of missing something, of messing up and being taken to task about it.

"The other killing?" asked Joel Hough.

"An individual from the Lansdowne. One Joe Tanner." Leah heard Speedy whistle and looked up. "Something to add, Speedy?"

"Joe Tanner, otherwise known as 'the driver,'" he told the team. "And he was employed by Slicer Shaw. Slicer isn't allowed to drive for health reasons, so Joe Tanner takes him everywhere. The two were close. There wouldn't be much going on in Slicer's life that Joe didn't know about. Very brave of whoever it was, taking out one of Slicer's own." Speedy chuckled.

"At this point we have no idea why Tanner was killed. Let's keep our fingers crossed that it isn't the beginning of a gang war," Leah told them. "We are short-handed for a couple days while the DCI and DC Harper are in Brighton. We will have to do the best we can. Later this morning we'll speak to Ray Shaw. Find out what Tanner was up to last night."

"He's unlikely to tell us anything useful, ma'am," Speedy told her. "He's well known for sorting his own problems."

"Nonetheless, make him a priority. I'd like to think that the two killings last night were unrelated, but my gut tells me they are. I want everything you can find on Adam Crompton. Any link to Slicer Shaw, no matter how tenuous, I want to know about it."

"How come we know the man's name?" asked Speedy.

"He was in the pub with a friend. He said in his statement that Crompton went to the loo, and when he didn't come back he went to look for him. He's given us the man's address. A uniformed PC went round there last night but there was no one in. Apparently his wife has been working nights at the hospital. I'll take a uniform and go speak to her myself."

"Must have been a shock, finding him like that." Joel Hough shuddered.

"According to the paramedics who attended, there was blood everywhere."

"And Tanner, ma'am? How did he get it?"

"Tanner was shot. One bullet in the back. Went through his heart. I will speak to DCI Greco later today and bring him up to speed. Forensics will get what they can from the bullet. We should know pretty soon if the gun has been used before."

Speedy picked up the Jamal Ali file off Grace's desk. "What I don't get is the connection. What do Ali and the other runner have to do with a man like Crompton? And Chorlton is across town from the Lansdowne."

"Whether we see it not, there is a link," Leah said. "Between the lot of them. DCI Greco wanted the reporter, Rouse, interviewing again, formally this time. We know he argued with Ali. Greco thinks he may have been chasing the lad for a story." She looked at Speedy. "Before you do anything else, bring him in, and take PC Dobbs with you. Once you've done that, ring me and then we'll meet up. First we'll visit the scene of the shooting, then we'll speak to Ray Shaw."

* * *

Speedy and Dobbs drove into the centre of Openshaw and parked up. The newspaper offices were in the shopping precinct. With luck someone would know where Rouse was.

The girl behind the reception desk was young, pretty and seemed more interested in playing a game on her mobile than anything else. "He hasn't rung in this morning," she said. "He's always like this when he's working on a story. He will be out mithering someone for information."

"Shouldn't he keep you informed?" asked Speedy. "What if he gets himself into a situation?"

The girl looked up at him and smiled. "You know our Mr Rouse then. He has a knack of rubbing folk up the wrong way. The editor keeps on telling him, but does he listen?" She shrugged. "Can't stand the man myself. Tony is far too full of himself. Thinks he's God's gift, when the truth is, he's a first-class loser."

Speedy chuckled. "Harsh words. Do you know what he's working on at the moment?"

"Tony has been following up on information he was given about some posh clinic in Chorlton. He won't let it drop. He is convinced there is a story there that's going to take him to the big time. Load of bollocks, if you ask me. It just means he can make himself scarce and no one asks awkward questions."

"Do you know any of the details?"

"Even if I did, it would be more than my job's worth to blab to you or anyone else." She smiled sweetly up at him and Dobbs. "Truth is, I know nowt, love. Tony's like that. Keeps everything close."

"Is there anyone else who'd know where I can find him? It is important." Speedy tried to charm her with a smile.

She looked in her desk diary. "You could ask Adam Crompton. He sometimes works with Tony. He's freelance, but Tony reckons he's good at wheedling stuff out of folk."

So there was their link! Crompton knew Rouse, worked with him in fact. That fitted. Crompton had been killed in a pub not far from the Rashid Clinic. Speedy kept his expression bland. "Work together much, did they?"

"Off and on. But they've been together a lot recently, as the expense claims will tell you."

"Do you know why?"

"No, but even if I did, I've already told you, I can't say."

Speedy looked around. "Smart offices."

"Crap part of town, though. I'd much rather be in the city centre. Much more going on and there's the shops in the dinner hour."

"Do you have another address for Rouse other than his mother's? We've already been there, but that's not where he lives all the time, is it?"

"Shouldn't really, but I suppose it's okay, you being police."

It was the one Rouse's mother had given Greco and Grace, a flat in an area of Manchester known as 'Spinningfields.' It looked as though a trip into the city was on the cards.

Once he and Dobbs were back in the car, Speedy rang Leah Wells. "He's not at work. They don't know where he is, ma'am, but Rouse knew Adam Crompton. Crompton did research for him. Rouse was interested in the Rashid Clinic, but he wouldn't tell his colleagues why. I'm about to try his address."

"Let me know if you find him. Given the location, the connection with Rouse could be the reason why Crompton was killed. Rouse may know something. We need to speak to the man as soon as."

That was all very well, but Leah didn't have the city traffic to deal with. Speedy hated every journey he made into Manchester these days. Tramlines seem to sprout up overnight, leaving entire swathes of Manchester centre no-go areas for cars. And the new one-way system around Piccadilly station had Speedy tearing his hair out.

"How the hell do folk do this every day?" he said, screeching to a halt just in time to stop them rear-ending a Mini.

Dobbs shook his head. "Can't understand it either. Easier to take a bus, sir."

They arrived in Spinningfields, outside a block of modern flats. "Reckon you have to have a bob or two to live around here," he told Dobbs. The block Rouse lived in hadn't been up long. Most of the apartments had balconies overlooking the river. "Rouse must be doing something right. It's Premier League territory this."

Rouse lived on the seventh floor, number seventy-three. They found a man and a woman banging on the reporter's door. "He didn't come back last night. The poor cat will be starving," the woman said. "You don't know where he's gone, do you?"

Speedy showed them his badge. "We're looking for him too. They told me at his office that Mr Rouse often does this."

"Yes, we know, but he usually leaves the key with us. We're his neighbours, and we feed Ghost. The cat. Tony loves that cat. He'd never just leave him uncared for."

"Is there someone who can let us in?" asked Speedy.

"We have a caretaker. He has an apartment on the ground floor. I'll ring him and ask him to come up."

A few minutes later the lift doors opened and the caretaker appeared. He didn't look pleased. "This is against procedure," he told them, shaking his head. He checked both men's badges carefully, despite the fact that Dobbs was wearing a uniform. After much handwringing on the part of the neighbours about the plight of the cat, he finally agreed to let them in.

The apartment was so sparsely furnished it hardly looked lived in. There were no photos or ornaments, not even cushions on the leather sofa. Speedy and Dobbs went into each room in turn. The fitted wardrobe in the bedroom held a single change of clothes. It didn't look as if Rouse spent much time here at all.

"See him often, do you?" Speedy asked the neighbours, who'd followed him in.

"He comes and goes. But he usually tells us. Leaves food for Ghost. He's a busy man. He works for the paper, you know."

Speedy didn't want to waste time listening to the details of Rouse's arrangements for his cat. He wanted to find the man, interview him, then meet up with DI Wells. But there was nothing here. No mail, nor paperwork of any sort lying around that would give him a clue as to Rouse's whereabouts.

Speedy was about to call it a day when he stuck his head around the bathroom door. There was a hole in the tilework on one of the walls. As Speedy went a bit closer he could see a fine spray of dried blood surrounding it. It looked very much like someone had been shot in here.

"We'll have to seal the place off," he told Dobbs. "Stay here and make sure no one comes in, then wait for forensics."

Adam Crompton had worked with Rouse. He was dead. What was the guessing that whoever had done him in had had a hand in this too?

* * *

"Different method," Leah Wells reminded him. "You say it looks like Rouse was shot. Crompton was stabbed. We mustn't get ahead of ourselves. We have no idea what went on in that flat, or if the blood is even Rouse's. We'll wait a while. See if he turns up, and what the forensic people have to say."

The two detectives had met on a piece of waste ground on the Lansdowne.

"Used to be the kid's playground," Speedy told her. "Nothing here now. The bastards have ripped up the equipment. No doubt the metal has long since been sold for scrap."

"Are you sure it's safe to leave the cars here?" Leah Wells looked around at the desolate tower blocks. "This isn't a pool car. It's my own."

"Risky, but I'll get one of the uniforms to watch them for us."

"Where are we going?"

"Ground floor, number nine, Argo House."

They walked across the cracked, crumbling concrete pathway towards a taped-off area.

"The shooting took place just outside the main doors to the block down there," a uniformed PC told them as they approached. "Scenes of Crime have done their stuff. Now they're inside the flat."

"We'll take a look anyway," Leah decided. She shuddered as they made their way along the litter-strewn deck. "Living here must be an acquired taste."

"Tanner won't have needed to, ma'am. He'd lived here all his life. Slicer will have paid him well. I expect he could afford better, but this was where he felt safe."

"Weird, if you ask me. Slicer is bound to have enemies."

"Not round here he doesn't," Speedy told her. "Folk are terrified of him."

A tall man in a coverall met them as they approached. "There's nothing inside. He was shot here, at the entrance and died where he fell."

"And you are . . . ?" asked Leah.

"Doctor Greg Pentland, the Duggan Centre."

"Anything in the flat to suggest a motive?" she asked. "Signs of robbery, or a break-in?"

"As I said, nothing," Greg Pentland confirmed. "But we do have footprints from outside. We've taken casts. There is a series of them coming towards the doorway and then running off again in that direction." He pointed towards Trojan House.

"So the killer could have been waiting for Tanner to return home?"

"It rained yesterday evening. The killer's shoes, or more likely trainers given the prints, were covered in dirt. I'd say your killer was standing over there." He pointed to where they had left their cars. "The ground is uneven, weeds have grown so when it rains it's muddy underfoot. He came in this direction, shot the victim then took off that way."

"Someone local, knew the layout of the estate."

"A grudge killing? Or perhaps we're back to the idea of a takeover," Leah suggested.

"Either way, it's not good. Slicer will want revenge," Speedy's eyes widened. "I certainly wouldn't want to be the one in that particular frame."

"We're not doing any good here. We should speak to the man himself."

Speedy checked his notebook for the address they had for Slicer. "The leafy suburbs of Didsbury it is then. Why don't I get one of the uniforms to take my pool car back and I'll come with you?"

Leah nodded.

"As long as you promise not to bite my head off." He grinned at her.

"This morning — sorry. I'd had McCabe on my back. He'd heard about the two killings overnight and wanted to help. It does my head in. He has every confidence in Greco — but me?" She threw her hands in the air. "I had to fight tooth and nail for my promotion. I thought I'd proved my worth on the last case I worked on at Central. I don't need McCabe shadowing me here."

"It is a tough case, and we don't know how long Greco and Grace will be gone," Speedy reminded her.

"Not you and all. Give me a break!"

Speedy watched Leah Wells stride away. She stopped briefly for a word with the PC at the entrance to Argo House and then made for her car. Sometimes she seemed fine, quite happy to have a joke at his expense, like at the Rashid Clinic. But it was becoming obvious that she couldn't handle any challenge to her ability.

Speedy climbed in beside her. "It's a fact. We're pushed, and like it or not, without Greco we're going to struggle."

"I don't want McCabe chucking his bright ideas at us. He'll take over, and expect us to go along with him. I know he's the super, but he can be a difficult bugger to work with."

"Didsbury is that way, incidentally."

Leah had just taken the wrong exit off the A34 roundabout.

"I don't know this part of town very well. I don't want you getting the idea that I'm a moody cow either."

"I didn't say that."

"It's written all over your face. But I'm not really. I work hard. I'm ambitious and I've nothing to stop me going for it. I have no ties. No husband, lover or kids to worry about. I'm lucky enough to have a straight run at this, and I intend to go to the top."

"No man in your life?" Speedy grinned.

"Don't go getting any bright ideas. You've got a woman, remember her? What's her name?"

"Michelle, but she won't last. She's a laugh, likes a good time, but she'll get fed up, they all do. It's the job."

"All I need to do is to keep at it. With the right breaks, I'll crack it. I wanted this post because it meant working with DCI Greco. He's got his problems but he's still one of the best. I want him to trust in my ability to get the job done. He won't do that if the minute he's not around, I have McCabe watching my every move."

"Snapping at the team isn't the way. You need us," Speedy reminded her. "Greco does have his problems. In the beginning I doubted he was ever going to fit in. But he does, and despite his odd ways, we like him."

"Particularly DC Harper." Leah gave a wry smile.

"They get on. She likes him, that's true, and I don't know how much it's reciprocated. Sometimes I think Greco isn't interested, but at other times they are as thick as thieves. Particularly when it comes to childcare." He laughed. "One of these days she'll see the light and look elsewhere — at me for instance."

"In your dreams, Sergeant. Grace has more sense."

"I'm not a bad catch! Good job, got my act together. I could go places."

"By my reckoning, we're here." Leah Wells ignored his last remark and pulled up outside a large red-brick detached house. "Lives in some style, our villain."

"This is a waste of time. We'll get nothing from him," Speedy told her.

"We have to go through the motions. Tanner worked for him. We've got to interview Shaw, or it will leave a gap in the investigation."

"Whatever you say, ma'am. But don't be surprised if he refuses to talk to us."

But much to Speedy's surprise, Ray 'Slicer' Shaw didn't refuse. He opened the door, knew exactly who they were and invited them in.

He launched straight in. "What are you doing about the bastard who killed my driver? Streets aren't safe these days. That estate should be torn down. You lot need to sort the drug dealing that goes on there too."

The man had some nerve. He was responsible for most of it! Speedy and Leah followed him into a palatial sitting room. "When did you last see Mr Tanner, sir?"

"Three days ago."

"He wasn't working for you last night then?"

"Can't you add up, copper? I said Tanner worked for me occasionally. When I go out he drives me. These days that's not very often." He frowned. "Health issues."

"Do you have any idea who would want to shoot Mr Tanner?" asked Leah.

"If I did, I'd say. I don't have much time for you lot normally, but Tanner was one of mine. I want whoever took him out catching. The man was gunned down in a public place. Someone must have seen something. That's your job. Find them and make them pay."

Chapter 11

Speedy and Leah Wells were back in the car.

"Slicer does have a point," said Speedy. "The Lansdowne is very public. Our problem is that no one is likely to come forward once they learn that our victim was none other than Slicer's driver."

"Ray Shaw wasn't like the hype. He came across as a reasonable chap."

"It was you who gave us the file," Speedy reminded her. "You know the truth. Underneath that veneer of respectability, he's a sadistic killer who harbours grudges. If he finds out that some poor bugger did see the shooting, he'll beat the crap out of them to get a name. I don't reckon much to our chances of getting anything after that."

"The club he owns, where is it?"

"Deansgate Locks," Speedy replied. "But not at this time of day, please! I've just negotiated my way around the city centre and it did my head in."

"Deansgate Locks is only a stone's throw away from Spinningfields, where Rouse lives."

"We will check it out. But that's best done at night when the place is open. It would be useful to know if Rouse was known there." Right now all Speedy wanted was to go back to the nick and get himself a strong mug of coffee. "Can I suggest that we see what forensics turn up first?"

Leah didn't appear convinced.

"I didn't ask how you got on with Crompton's wife this morning." Speedy asked.

"She was gutted, as you'd expect. She identified the body but couldn't come up with any reason why anyone would want him dead. And they do know each other, Slicer and our reporter. Before he went, Greco left me a comprehensive report of his findings so far. According to what Rouse's mother told Greco, they drank together. So Rouse may well have been to that club. Make that visit a priority," Leah instructed.

"I bet Rouse only talks to Slicer when he's after something. I'll get Joel to look into their background. They are a similar age. Did Crompton's wife know what her husband was working on?" asked Speedy.

"She told me that he kept his work to himself. Crompton maintained that the less she knew, the safer she was. She suggested that we look at his notebook, but we didn't find one."

"Good advice from Crompton. Given the killer's MO I think we can assume he took the notebook along with everything else. We need to find Rouse, or what's happened to him. Problem is, we don't know who he's upset."

"Okay, we'll go back and see what the others have turned up," Leah agreed.

Much to Speedy's relief, she turned towards the Mancunian Way. That would take them to Ashton Old Road and from there it was only a stone's throw to the station.

* * *

"Speedy and I have spoken to Ray Shaw, and Leah spoke to Adam Crompton's widow. Not that we're any the wiser. Tony Rouse has disappeared, leaving what looks like a bullet hole on his bathroom wall and a trail of blood. Joel — have you got anything for us from the CCTV?"

Leah Wells updated the incident board as she waited for Joel to find the snippet of film he wanted to show them. She was frustrated at the lack of solid information. At this rate they would have spent the day going around in circles, and that wouldn't look good on the report McCabe had asked for.

"I think this is the same character I picked up outside the car park." Joel pointed to the computer screen. "This is from the CCTV at the Bull's Head. See how he keeps to the perimeter, head down, trying to blend into the shadow cast by that tall hedge. The clothing is the same too."

"The quality isn't good. We never get a good look at his face. But it does look like the same person. Has forensics come up with anything?" asked Leah.

"Doctor Greg Pentland rang. Something about footprints. He wants you to ring him back."

Leah Wells disappeared into Greco's office to use the phone.

"How tall, d'you reckon?" Speedy asked Joel.

"Quite tall. You can gauge by the hedge. A few inches short of six foot, I'd say."

"Tall, slight, never looks up at the cameras . . ."

"Deliberate. Knows the cameras are there and doesn't want to be recognised."

"That could mean we might know him."

Leah came out of Greco's office. "Greg Pentland says the footprints were from a long, slim foot — no smaller than size ten."

Speedy shrugged. "So our killer has big feet. I don't see how that's relevant."

She nodded. Speedy looked again at the film Joel had on his computer screen. "He's young. Probably not yet twenty and still growing, if his feet are anything to go by."

"Those boys were killed in cold blood. It took skill and nerve." Leah shook her head. "What are they teaching them at school these days?"

"It's not what they learn in school, Leah. It's what they pick up on the street that's dangerous. He's young, but skilled. There was no rough stuff. No one put up a fight. Like we've said before, the kid is a shadow. No one notices. He blends, kills and then walks away."

Leah was frustrated. This was all conjecture, and McCabe wouldn't go for it. They had to come up with something better. What they desperately needed was a break. "I'm nipping out for a bit. Anything comes up, I'm on my mobile."

"Want company?" asked Speedy.

"No. Best I keep you lot out of it."

Leah took the blue Vauxhall. It was older than the rest and had numerous knocks and scratches. No one would give it a second look, and that was a distinct advantage where she was going. Travelling along Gorton Road, she took the turn onto the Lansdowne. Swinging round the back of Trojan House, she drove for a further half mile. Sprawled out in front of her was one of the largest social housing estates in this part of Manchester. Built in the fifties, it was in desperate need of refurbishment. There wasn't a patch of green. The space that had once been laid out to grass was now nothing but a huge bare scar in the expanse of concrete. Slap bang in the centre of all this deprivation was a pub — the Grapes. Anyone passing who didn't know, would think the place was closed. There were bars on every window, and the walls and door were liberally daubed with graffiti. But the Grapes did a brisk trade. It was the haunt of every dealer and crook within a mile of it, and that included the Lansdowne.

Leah parked the car where she could keep an eye on it. She quickly changed her shoes, swapping her black flatties for a pair of shiny red heels. She swiped lipstick across her mouth, pulled up the collar of her jacket against the wind and made for the entrance.

The place was basic. The tables and chairs were made of wood and metal and there wasn't a padded seat or cushion in sight.

Leah strode across to the bar. She was chewing gum, her hands in her jeans pockets, and she slouched forward. In the few seconds it had taken her to park up and walk to the pub, she'd undergone a complete transformation. Leah reckoned it was all in the stance and the attitude. "Roman in?"

The barman nodded to a side room. "Busy. They've got a game on."

"Get him." Leah picked up the half pint of beer he'd put in front of her. "Go on, he won't mind. He's on a promise."

The barman leered at her. "What about giving me a bit of what he's getting?"

"Fond of your bollocks, are you?"

He disappeared to return almost immediately, followed by a heavily built man.

"Come to see good old Uncle Roman, eh? Must want something." He laughed, and slapped her across her rear end.

Leah kissed his cheek. "You know me, see a good thing and I can't keep away."

Still laughing, he led her to a table by the window, out of earshot. "Must be serious to bring you to this shithole."

"It is. I need something on the Knifeman," she whispered. "The joker who's new, and good with a blade. You must have heard."

Roman McLaughlin was in his mid-sixties. He was a large, ugly man with a wicked scar running down his right cheek. He had a past, and he'd been inside. Leah didn't know his real first name. He'd been given the nickname 'Roman' because of the shape of his nose. They'd met five years ago when Leah had been working a case at Central. Roman had witnessed the torching of a friend's house. His family had been asleep inside and they'd stood no chance. The brutal killing had sickened him. Shortly after that he'd approached Leah, and he'd proved very useful ever since. He knew a lot of bad people, and they still thought of him as one of their own. Problem was, he insisted on always meeting at the Grapes. He maintained it was safer for them both. Working out of Central meant that Leah wasn't known here. Anyone who saw them together simply thought she was his latest tart. But given her recent promotion to the area, that would have to change.

"You don't look well, Roman." Leah noticed the grey pallor of his cheeks. He wheezed when he spoke, and each sentence ended with a harsh cough. He drank too much, smoked too much and as far as Leah could tell, hardly ever left this place. "You need to take care of yourself or you'll end up in hospital."

"Don't worry about me, love. I've plenty of life left in me yet."

"The Knifeman, you've heard of him?"

"Word has it that the Knifeman is Slicer's new pet."

The Knifeman was working for Slicer Shaw! Did that make sense? Surely he had plenty of thugs on his payroll already? "I don't understand. Slicer isn't short of muscle."

"He wanted someone clean. These killings are related, special. Don't ask me how or why because I don't know, not for sure. Once the job is done, Slicer will walk away, his operation intact, but I bet we don't see your knifeman again."

"You think Slicer will get rid?"

"Yes. This is a one-off job. After that — the kid's expendable."

"In that case, can I presume that the two lads were not drug runners?"

"You presume right. But I've no idea who the poor bastards were. No one knows."

"Do you have any idea what's going on?" Leah asked him.

"I heard a whisper. Nothing concrete, you understand." Roman leaned in closer. "People trafficking is what I was told."

That was something they hadn't considered, but they should have.

"The lads were trying to get away and had to be silenced."

Leah smiled at him. "Thanks, Roman, that makes sense. Who told you this?"

He pulled a face. "If I tell you, little lady, and he finds out, I'll get nowt else."

"Take the risk, Roman. I need this case to break."

"Tony Rouse. I was drinking with him a few nights ago. He's usually a tight-lipped sod but he'd had a few and couldn't keep his gob shut. Didn't say much, mind you, but just enough. He's chasing a story and reckons it's big. Trafficking on a grand scale. The people doing this have it all worked out. The kids, the method, and places to sell them on once they're in the UK."

"Did he say where the kids were destined for?"

"Not exactly. But it is bound to be some backstreet sweatshop or factory where the staff get next to nowt."

"Did Rouse say that?"

"He hinted. That's what it usually is."

They had to find Rouse, bring him in. Get him to tell them what he knew.

"Do you know where Rouse is holed up?"

Roman shook his head. "I reckon he's got in too deep. Attracted the attention of the wrong people. If he's still alive he'll be difficult to find."

"Slicer's driver was shot last night. What was that about?"

"I'm not sure. There are a lot of rumours doing the rounds. It is hinted that Slicer wants the big man's patch."

"He wants to take over from Costello?" Leah was genuinely surprised. She didn't think he had the balls.

Roman nodded. "The shooting, killing the driver, was Costello fighting back. Marking Slicer's card."

"Are you sure?"

"Like I say, that's what is going around. I have no reason to doubt it. Slicer Shaw has played second fiddle to Costello for years. People are saying he's had enough."

"Any idea who he is, this kid with the blade?"

Roman McLaughlin smiled at her. "No, I don't have a name. No one does."

* * *

The notebook was full of nonsense. Words and funny little squiggles Mickey didn't understand. Crompton was some sort of investigator and he'd been working for Tony Rouse. Some words did stand out. The Rashid Clinic for starters. So it had to be significant. The two dead boys, the pair he'd killed, had been there. It said so in the notes. One name was underlined — Jamal Ali. What was so special about him? It might be nonsense to Mickey, but was it worth money? No good asking Slicer. He was best avoided until he'd got over the driver's death. So who? Perhaps that hack, the man Crompton had worked for? He would pay. Either that or Mickey would threaten to send it to the police. On the back page was Rouse's name and mobile number. Mickey tapped it in. Nothing, the thing was dead.

Rouse was up to his neck in this. But how to find him? This notebook had to hold a clue. Mickey glanced at the clock and then studied the reflection of the skinny kid who looked back at him from the glass.

Then he had an idea. He smiled. There was someone who might be able to help.

Chapter 12

The Italian restaurant was in a pleasant little square at the confluence of several narrow lanes. It was early evening, and the late autumn sun had brought folk out. People sat outside drinking and chatting. Inside, the place was just as busy.

Grace looked around. "Nice. Wish this was on our doorstep after work. Very different from the Gorton Arms."

Greco went straight to the bar and asked for Amani Ali. The young man serving looked at him with suspicion.

"What do you want with her?" he asked.

"She knows we are coming. My name is Greco." He omitted the 'DCI.' The fewer who knew the reason for their visit, the better. The barman disappeared to return a few minutes later with a young woman. Greco put her in her mid-twenties. She was wearing a plain black dress that covered her arms and legs, plus a headscarf. The barman spoke to her in what Greco guessed was Arabic, and then gestured to a room off the main eating area.

"Is it alright for you to take a few minutes off?" Greco asked. "We can wait until you come off shift if you'd rather."

Amani Ali said nothing. Once the three of them were inside the small room, she closed the door, and nodded at Grace. "Who is this?"

"DC Grace Harper. I thought you might be more comfortable if she was present," he explained.

"Okay, she can stay," Amani said.

"You've seen the photo of our victim. It isn't very good, I'm afraid. Is there anything you can tell me about Jamal that will confirm that it's him?"

"Jamal has an old scar where he had his appendix out. But the big thing is his feet. They are different sizes." She smiled. "We always teased him about it as children. My parents had to get his shoes specially made. Fortunately they were well off. Before the war, that was." She lowered her head.

So it was him. Now the grim task of confirming the news. "I'm afraid it is your brother who was killed, Miss Ali. We are both very sorry."

She stiffened. "Where is his body?"

"He is still in the morgue." Greco saw her face fall. "The forensic people will do tests. It might be possible for them to tell us where Jamal had been, or what he'd been doing prior to his death," he explained.

"You will not find anything. The men who killed Jamal are evil, and they are clever. They trade in misery."

"What do you mean, Amani?"

"Jamal will have been given the clothing you found him in. Apart from his shoes, the rest will tell you nothing."

Greco recalled Roxy Atkins saying that his clothing hadn't fitted properly.

"His shoes have proved useful," Grace agreed.

"Who gave him the clothes he was wearing?" asked Greco.

"I suspect the men who took him. He was kept prisoner."

"Do you know who they were? Their names, or where we can find them?"

"No," she told Greco. "But Jamal was terrified. When he first came to England he was brought here to Brighton. The men who brought him got him a job in a hotel. He was told to stay put and not to tell people who he was or where he'd come from. But he rang me. I was living with a friend in London. I came here and found work to be near Jamal. We saw each other. He was okay, earning a little money, and he had somewhere to live. But then one day he rang me. He told me that the men were taking him away. He said there was no way he could escape because they were watching him. If he tried to run, they would kill him. He wanted me to help him, but there was nothing I could do."

"Do you have other family in the UK?" asked Greco.

"No. I have been in the UK for one year only. My friends in London helped me to find this job in Brighton. The pay is not good, but I get a room upstairs and no one asks awkward questions. It will do for now."

Greco wondered if that meant she was here illegally but he wasn't going to ask her.

"Did Jamal say anything about where these men were taking him?"

"He said Manchester, but he could give me no address."

"Couldn't he get help? Speak to someone, tell them what was going on?" asked Grace.

"That was not possible. The men were always with him. Jamal was here illegally. If he went to the authorities he would have been sent back. Our village has been razed to the ground. There is nothing left for him, nothing for anyone. Before he was brought here he'd lived for five months in the camp at Calais. He was only seventeen years old. I tried then to get him to the UK, so that he could join me in London. But I have no money. Jamal was ill. That place is not fit for children. He was desperate, and so was I. When he was offered the chance of work here in Brighton, he took it."

"Where is your home, Amani?" asked Grace.

"My family is in Syria. But it is not safe to return. When the soldiers came to our village, they took Jamal and his friends. For weeks we did not know what had happened to him, even if he was still alive. We were desperate. Then we learned he was in France. I don't know how, but he made it across the Turkish border. Soon after he got a lift in a truck belonging to an Eastern European man. For a fee he dropped him in Calais. Our family was relieved, but they hadn't seen what conditions are like there. I was already living in the UK so our parents begged me to arrange for Jamal to come here too. But I couldn't do that without money."

"So how exactly did he get here?"

"The man who dropped him in Calais arranged it. He is often in the camp. Jamal told me that he regularly brought people to the UK. But he wanted young, fit men only. Those who could work and were healthy."

"Did you or Jamal have to pay him?" asked Grace.

"No, and that surprised me. Despite asking for money to bring him from Turkey, all he wanted in return for taking Jamal across the channel was a blood sample. Then he had to wait a few days to see if he had been chosen. They have brought many young men here to the UK this way. Now I know why." She sighed deeply. "They are brought here to work, to work until they drop."

Grace looked at Greco. "How do they travel here from Calais?"

"In lorries. Jamal told me that the one he travelled in was big and safe. They leave from Calais and take the ferry to Dover. He did not tell me much but the lorries are adapted so that the young men can remain hidden. They were given food and water during the journey. The man and his friends have been doing this for months. They have brought dozens of boys across in this way."

Greco's face was grim. It was possible that they'd bribed someone at Border Control in Dover to let them through. "What happens to the boys when they arrive in England?"

"I don't know. They work all over the country. Jamal said it depended on the test results."

"The blood test?" Greco thought this odd. He'd supposed cold, hard cash was the only criteria.

"Yes, and once they are here there are other medical tests, to check that they are healthy I guess. Then they are found jobs. Jamal was lucky, he was brought here to Brighton. Some of the others were sent to work in a factory in London. For a while we were okay. I saw Jamal often. But then the men wanted more tests. The man who'd brought him here wanted him to go to Manchester. Jamal rang me three times. The first time he told me what had happened to him. He sounded fine, said he'd be back. But the second time he was terrified. He said the whole thing was about getting the boys here to become nothing more than slaves, but that it was even worse for him. I didn't know what he meant. I wanted him to tell me everything but Jamal said they would kill me if I knew. He didn't know what would happen to him. Several days went by before I heard from him again. The last time we spoke he was crying. He told me that they were going to kill him. He asked me for money to help him get away. I asked him about the job. Jamal said that there was no job. The man who took him said it was for something far more important." She fell silent. "I never spoke to Jamal again."

"Do you know what that important something was?"

She shook her head.

"Why are you so frightened, Amani?" Greco asked gently.

"Because a man came here to the restaurant, looking for Jamal. He was not a nice man. He hurt me." She showed them a bruise on her lower right arm. "I told him Jamal wasn't here, but he didn't believe me."

"Did you go to the police, ask for help?"

She looked at Grace. "No, they can't help. If I get into trouble they will send me home."

"You're not in trouble, Amani," Greco assured her. "We want to find the person that killed your brother." He paused. "Jamal is not the only young man who has died. Another youth has been murdered in the same way. Do you have any idea who he might be?"

The young woman shook her head. "Jamal never mentioned any names."

"Can you describe the man who came here and threatened you?" asked Grace.

"Marco, he serves in the bar, said he had a Northern accent. He was a big man. His stomach stuck out. When he got angry, his face went red."

Could be anyone, but Greco had an idea. That description fitted Tony Rouse. "Can you recall exactly what date this was?" He'd noticed the CCTV camera above the counter.

"Four days ago. It was about four thirty in the afternoon."

"I'd like to speak to Marco."

Amani nodded. "I'll get him."

Grace waited until she was out of the room. "What are you thinking?"

"Tony Rouse. The CCTV will help confirm it. We'll need to speak to the local force."

Greco took his mobile from his jacket pocket and tapped in Joel Hough's number. "Joel, will you text me a photo of Tony Rouse as quick as you can."

"If Amani recognises him, what then?"

"If she does, it means Rouse knows a lot more than he's told us. That he knew who Jamal was all along. Rouse could easily become our prime suspect."

Amani returned with Marco in tow. "We have CCTV but we don't keep the recordings for long, a couple of days, no more. So the day you are interested in is gone, I'm afraid."

At that moment Greco's mobile pinged. "Is this the man?" He showed them both the image.

Amani Ali cast a wary glance at Marco and nodded. "Yes, that is the man." Marco echoed her words.

"Thanks," Greco told them. "We know this individual." He looked at Amani. "He won't bother you again."

"Will you speak to me again?" she asked.

"Probably tomorrow. Will you be here?"

Amani nodded.

Greco and Grace walked out into the square.

Greco was frowning. "Rouse was chasing a story. More than likely, one about illegal immigrants. What Amani told us about the boys is worrying."

"We've stumbled into something big and nasty, haven't we? In fact, if we're not careful, we could become targets ourselves."

Greco looked at Grace. The expression on her face told him she wasn't joking, and she was right. "The men who transport from Calais bring some of them here. We need a word with the local force."

Chapter 13

"It's a line of enquiry we can pursue." As soon as she returned to the nick, Leah had met with the team.

Speedy looked doubtful. "People trafficking, ma'am? Is your source sure? Given we're dealing with the scrotes from the Lansdowne, good old-fashioned drug dealing is a safer bet."

"It's what I've been told, Speedy."

"So why the Knifeman?"

"Because Slicer Shaw wants someone new. Someone who's MO isn't known to us, is untraceable and can be got rid of once it's over."

"Have you told Greco?" he asked.

Leah Wells shook her head. "I wanted to bring the team up to speed first."

Speedy frowned. "He won't thank you for keeping him out of the loop."

"I'm sure DCI Greco has enough on his plate right now," she replied tersely.

"Are you sure your snout knows what he's on about?"

"Quite sure. Why, what's troubling you?"

"People trafficking. That takes us to a whole new level."

"We can't ignore it." Speedy's negative comments were beginning to annoy Leah.

"What about Slicer wanting to take over from Costello?" Joel Hough asked. "That'll give us no end of problems if it's true. We'll have carnage, and not just on the Lansdowne either."

"The problem is, we don't know who this rival is. We might suspect but we've got nothing we can pin on anybody," Leah replied.

"If it is true we'll have evidence soon enough," Speedy joked.

"I know that, Speedy. We need to find Rouse. He is the key to this. He knows far more than he's let on. Anything from forensics?"

"Not yet," Joel replied.

Leah looked at the clock. "It's getting late. We'll resume tomorrow. Forensics first thing, Joel. Get uniform to keep an eye on Rouse's flat too, just in case he goes back there. We have his mobile number — get a list of calls and go through them."

"If we go with the trafficking theory, it means the lads are being brought here for a reason," said Speedy. "We should look at the places they could end up in. Sweatshops, small factories round the backstreets."

"This is the right part of town for them," Joel agreed. "Remember that case last year? A small factory in Beswick producing T-shirts. Full of illegals from China working all hours for nothing but a crust."

"Can I have a word before you go?" Leah asked Speedy once the others had left. "Are you up for a visit to Slicer's club tonight?"

"With you, ma'am?" he asked, surprised.

"No, that would look a bit too full on. If Slicer is there he'd spot us straight away. I was thinking you and your young lady."

"Okay, won't do any harm, and Michelle will love it."

* * *

"Where do you want to eat?" Grace asked.

"I thought back at the hotel." It hadn't occurred to Greco that they'd eat anywhere else. "They serve dinner until nine, so there is plenty of time."

Grace cocked her head. "Don't you fancy fish and chips on the pier instead? There's a bar, we could get a drink too."

It loomed ahead of them, a huge rectangular shape that looked almost like it was bouncing in the twilight. It was the last place he wanted to eat. The loud music and garish neon lights grated on his nerves. It smelled strongly of fried donuts and chip fat. "I've a couple of calls to make and a deal of thinking to do. But don't let me stop you," he replied.

"An hour won't hurt, Stephen. It's been a long, hard day." Grace took hold of his arm, tugging him along. "What happened to chilling, Greco? Of having a good time for a change?"

An obvious clash of opinions about what constituted having a *good time*, Greco thought.

"I'm fine as I am, Grace." He looked down at the manicured hand on his lower arm. Why couldn't he just go with this, relax a bit? Pat was right. Grace was okay. She could be fun to be with, and she was good-looking too. He should be flattered that she put so much effort into winning him over.

"Okay, the hotel it is then," she agreed reluctantly. "But after dinner you're going to help me make a dent in that bottle of vodka I brought with me."

He stepped away from her. "Oh no, I am not! We've been there before, remember?" Grace giggled. "And I don't want reminding, thank you."

"You got drunk — rare for you, but it loosened your tongue. We talked well into the night as I recall. And you actually laughed a bit before you crashed on my sofa. Nothing happened. You left my place that morning, your virtue intact." She giggled again. "It was a missed opportunity, though. When I think about what I could have done!" She nudged him. "A quick pic of you in my dressing gown, for example. Where would your credibility be then, newly appointed DCI?" There was a wicked grin on Grace's face.

He looked at her in genuine horror. "You didn't?"

She folded her arms. "Not telling. But come on the pier with me and eat, and I promise I won't do anything rash." She took hold of his hand.

"I'm not eating fish and chips."

"So you say, but you weren't coming on this pier with me either, a few minutes ago. Now look what's happened."

The planks they were walking on looked dodgy, and Greco could see the water below. "Are you sure this is safe? There are a lot of people on here. Will it take the weight?" The pier was buzzing with activity. They walked past a row of stalls, all selling tatty souvenirs. Grace pulled him into an arcade full of slot machines.

"Course it's safe. Want to chance your luck?"

Greco shook his head. The place was packed. There must be a fortune being spent in here, he thought, and mostly by kids. Grace darted behind one of those boards that you stick your head through to have your photo taken.

"A witch, how apt," Greco said, and took a snap of her on his mobile.

"It'll be Halloween soon. They have a 'Fear on the Pier' event. Shame we won't be here."

He looked at his phone. "I've got a missed called from DI Wells. All this noise going on, I didn't hear it ring."

"Never mind her for now. Get your bod back here and I'll take one of you."

She had that look on her face again. Grace wasn't taking no for an answer tonight. Photos taken, Greco finally rang Leah and spent the next five minutes swapping updates. They both agreed that given what they'd each discovered, they were definitely looking at people trafficking.

"I put salt and vinegar on." Grace handed him the open fish and chips in their greasy paper. "We'll sit on that bench at the end."

He looked at the food. He hadn't seen it being served. He hoped whoever had dished this up had clean hands, and that the stall's standard of hygiene was up to scratch.

"Try it, Stephen. Nothing on there is going to do you any harm."

"It's a bit breezy out here."

"It's mid-October, what d'you expect? The wind won't kill you, just ruffle your hair a bit, that's all."

They sat and ate their supper as the sky darkened and the moon rose high in the night sky above them.

Grace smiled at him. "I think this is quite romantic. And, go on, you are having fun. Not had a moan out of you in five minutes."

"These weren't bad actually." Greco screwed up the fish and chip paper tightly and threw it in the bin. "Sorry I'm so damn boring."

"I don't think you're boring, Stephen." She thought for a minute. "You just need retraining, that's all."

"Cheeky woman! Have you forgotten that we're working, and I'm your DCI?"

"If you keep reminding me, I won't get the chance. Back to the hotel now, is it?"

"We should. It's getting late. Leah's been given some information. She thinks it's people trafficking too. Tomorrow I'll speak to Border Control."

"That'll mean dropping Amani Ali in it. Don't you think she's suffered enough?"

"We don't have much choice. We've no idea how many more young men are in the same situation as Jamal. Someone has to put a stop to this."

"We don't know for sure that she's here legally, Stephen. We could warn her. If she does have a problem, that gives her a chance to leave, go back to London."

"We'll go and have another word in the morning."

The hotel wasn't far. By the time they returned, dinner was over and the main lounge was full. "Fancy that drink?" Greco asked her.

Grace popped her head around the door. "The bar here is crowded, and the one at the side is full of youngsters. There's always the minibar and the vodka I brought."

"Let me ring home and speak to Pat, and then I'll join you."

* * *

Speedy sat in the Gorton Arms with Michelle snuggled up close, her arms around his neck. She was sobbing. "He came out of nowhere and I'll swear he had a knife."

"On the Lansdowne, you say?"

"There was no one about. It was so dark and scary. I can't go back to that flat. I reckon folk know I'm seeing a copper. You know what that means round here. I'll be a target for all-comers."

"Did you actually see the knife, Michelle?"

She pouted at him. "You're angry, I can tell. You think this is my fault."

"No, that's not what I'm saying. But did you see the knife?"

"Not really." She wriggled on the seat. "But he looked as if he had one. He looked dodgy to me. It's possible it was the Knifeman you're looking for. The one that killed the kid."

"I doubt it." Speedy knew that the villain they were after had specific targets, and it was highly unlikely that Michelle was one of them.

89

"You don't believe me, do you? You think I'm making it up."

"No, I don't." He stroked the blonde hair from her face. "You were frightened by some bloke, but it wasn't who we're after."

She took another swallow of her drink. "Could have been. You don't know. You weren't with me."

"I do know." He looked around. Speedy didn't want anyone from the station hearing him. "Turns out our knifeman is after specific targets."

"Do you know who he is?"

"Not yet, but it won't be long."

"I could know him," she realised suddenly. "He could live on the Lansdowne. I know most folk on the estate. Is anyone else involved in the murders?"

Speedy didn't want to discuss the case with Michelle, but he wanted to reassure her that she was quite safe. "We want to find that reporter, Tony Rouse. He's gone to ground. Well, either that or he's been hurt. We don't know which. It's possible he's involved."

Michelle was wide-eyed with curiosity. "What makes you think he's been hurt? My mum went out with him once. He can be a right laugh."

"If you see him, be sure to let me know. He could be in danger."

"A bloke got shot last night outside Argo House," she told him soberly. "That estate isn't safe anymore."

"That was a gang-related thing."

"Are you sure? What gangs? The kids who hang around by the bins?"

"No, the shooting was down to a falling out among those who run the gangs. Nothing for you to worry about."

"I'm still not going back. Can I come and stay with you?"

Ordinarily Speedy wouldn't have minded. In fact, he'd have been flattered. But Michelle was so full on. She was noisy, messy, and she couldn't cook, so in effect she was a massive distraction. But he couldn't refuse. She was afraid, and it was known that she was seeing him. That made him feel responsible. "Okay, we'll go back to your place together and pick up what you need."

Michelle hugged him and planted a big kiss on his cheek.

"Where was it you wanted to go?"

"A club in Deansgate Locks," he told her.

"Do you mind if we don't? I'd much rather go back to yours and have an early night. I've had a nasty fright. I need some wine, and a cuddle."

How could he refuse? So much for the research. The club would have to wait until another night.

* * *

"I'm not measuring these, you know, and that's four you've had already."

"I wasn't counting." Greco smiled at her.

"If you go getting drunk again, don't blame me."

"It's your vodka we're drinking," he reminded her, shaking the bottle. "You brought it with you to drink, and there isn't a lot left."

"Minibar?"

Greco felt more relaxed than he had in months. Grace had put the radio on low. He'd removed his jacket and tie and relaxed back onto the soft pillows of the double bed.

She handed him a glass. "Whiskey and soda to finish, and that's your lot."

He downed the amber liquid. The clock said it was only ten thirty, but he needed to sleep. Tomorrow would be another long day.

"Your room is next door." Grace prodded him gently.

Her voice was soft, gentle, and the perfume she wore brought a smile to his lips. It was familiar. Suzy had worn it too. Pat was right. Grace was a very attractive young woman. He'd been mad not to pay more attention before.

"Come on, Stephen." She nudged him, but his eyes were closed. "I'm having a shower. You've got until I've finished, then I'll throw you out if I have to."

"You've plied me with drink again."

"No one had your arm up your back."

She was leaning over him. He could feel her long hair tickling his cheek.

"Ten minutes, then you're gone, Greco — understand?"

He opened his eyes and nodded. But there was no way that was going to happen.

Chapter 14

Day 4

Greco's head was pounding. The clock said six thirty in the morning. He should make a move. But drinking last night with Grace had left him with a hangover from hell. Rubbing his eyes, he rolled over in an attempt to get up. Immediately a hand snatched the duvet back. He heard a soft groan. He inhaled sharply, blinked his tired eyes a couple of times, then gently lifted the duvet. Grace Harper was asleep beside him! Worse than that, they were both starkers. His heart sank and panic set in. What had he done? This was all wrong! He had to get out. This was a long way from simply crashing on her sofa like last time.

She grabbed his arm and pulled him back. "Not so fast, lover boy. It's rude to shag and run."

"We didn't!" he protested, his brain racing. Why couldn't he remember?

"Oh yes, we did," Grace said. "For a bloke so intent on being just my friend, and such a goody two-shoes, there was no stopping you."

Grace hadn't opened her eyes. Her long blonde hair was loose and splayed over the pillow. She looked lovely, so relaxed and at ease with herself. So very different from him.

"Want some coffee?" he asked feebly.

She smiled and rolled onto her front. "I thought you'd never ask. I'm so warm and comfy, I don't want to move."

"We'll have to soon. Things to do, remember?"

Greco slipped out from under the duvet and wrapped himself in her dressing gown.

"Mine!" Grace giggled, watching him. "You've forgotten, this is my room."

"I can't go out onto the corridor in my birthday suit, can I?" He only had what he'd worn yesterday. No fresh clothes, no washbag.

"Stick those on." She nodded at the pile of clothes lying on the chair.

"I always shower first and put on fresh clothes each day." He sounded almost petulant. But he couldn't help how he was. It was all part of the OCD ritual.

"Make the coffee and I'll get your stuff for you. You can shower here too."

"The staff will know I've not slept in there."

"Rough the bed up a bit. Stop stressing about everything. What does it matter what folk think?"

That was something else. Would Grace tell the rest of the team what had happened between them? He looked at her, and it felt as if he were seeing Grace for the first time. Previously Suzy and their relationship had clouded the issue, but not anymore. Pat had seen it. She'd met Grace a number of times, and thought she was a woman he should get to know better.

"What happened last night . . ." he began.

She sat up. "I can see the cogs working, Stephen. Get that kettle on and we'll do a deal."

She was laughing at him.

"What sort of deal?"

Grace tilted her head to one side. "I'll keep my mouth shut. That is what you want, isn't it? You're not ready to go public yet?"

Go public? What did she think this was? "I'm not ready for any of this yet. It's too soon after—"

"Don't say it, Stephen — that really is boring."

Greco knew it was, but it hadn't stopped him from saying it. "Kettle's on. I'll go next door." He pulled her dressing tighter around himself. "Shower and dress. If you want coffee, you'll have to make it yourself."

He was confused. He didn't know what to think or feel. After months of convincing himself that he wasn't interested, he'd gone and slept with Grace anyway. Suddenly the goal posts had shifted. He couldn't understand what had changed.

He took his time getting ready. The thought of having to face Grace over the breakfast table was winding him up. He made a quick phone call to Border Control. A further call to another official called Raymond Hope was organised for later on that morning. That sorted, he rang Pat.

"Having a nice time?" she asked.

"It's not a holiday," he reminded her.

"You sound stressed, Stephen. Something happened?"

There was no way he could tell her. "It's just work. Tillyflop okay?"

"She's fine, eating her breakfast. Want a word?"

Not even chatting to his daughter could shift the thoughts of Grace. She filled his head. When he closed his eyes, he could see her lying there naked in the bed they'd shared. This was going to take some sorting.

* * *

"The good news is that it isn't human blood," Leah Wells announced to the team. Present for the briefing were

Speedy, Joel Hough and PC Gareth Dobbs. "According to Greg Pentland from the Duggan, it belonged to a pig."

She'd written all the new information on the board. McCabe would drop in later and, despite having nothing concrete, at least it looked impressive.

"So how does that happen? The spray was halfway up the wall," Speedy said.

"When we locate Mr Rouse, we'll ask him."

"Was it even a bullet hole?" asked Speedy.

"Yes, someone had used a gun in there. The bullet was found lodged in the wall."

"Rouse does have a gun licence," said Joel.

"So Rouse, or someone, destroys the décor in the bathroom, then sprays pig's blood on the tiles to make it look like he's been shot?"

Leah shrugged. "It looks that way."

"But he'd realise we'd find out the truth pretty quick. He's a lot of things, but he isn't stupid."

"It bought him some time, Speedy," Leah suggested. "Enough time to disappear. Word will have been out within an hour of you visiting his apartment and finding that blood. Rouse's enemies will think he's dead. Meanwhile, he legs it."

"So he set it up. He could be anywhere, in that case."

Joel Hough looked up from his monitor. "We do have something. His mobile phone number. We might catch up with him that way."

"Good call, Joel. Get on it." Leah hadn't meant right away, but Joel's attention was already back on the screen.

"If we're going with people trafficking, who do we suspect is behind it?" Speedy asked. "Until Jamal Ali escaped and got himself murdered, we were none the wiser. This is a well-planned operation. Folk are being brought in and we've no idea how, or for what purpose."

"That's not strictly true, Speedy," Leah reminded him. "DCI Greco has been told that people are being brought in by lorry. Young men, teenage kids from the camp in Calais."

"The camp is being wound up. So that won't last."

"The details are sketchy. But some of those boys were brought to our area. Jamal's sister told Greco that her brother had to undergo tests to ensure that he was healthy."

"Healthy enough to work in some backstreet sweatshop?" asked Speedy.

"We've no idea. But Jamal Ali had more than one set of tests. After which he was deemed to be 'special' and brought to Manchester."

"And we've no idea what was so special about him?"

"I'm afraid not. But I suspect Tony Rouse was onto something. He was tailing Jamal. For all we know he'd been watching him for days. What do you all think?"

"The Rashid Clinic. Perhaps they were responsible for these tests. The name keeps cropping up. We should look at it a little closer," Speedy suggested.

"It's a long shot. I can't work out why they'd be involved. They have no need for slave labour."

"It's worth another visit though, don't you think?"

"Okay, take PC Dobbs, go have another word. But tread carefully. We have nothing concrete on them. It's Rouse who thinks they are involved, but we don't know if they are or not." Leah's eyes flicked to Joel who was tapping away on his computer. Had he even been listening? she wondered. The young DC was keen but far too fond of doing his own thing. "Joel, are you up to speed with this?"

"Yes, ma'am." He looked up and then around at the others. "I'm just checking Rouse's phone records. He made a call an hour ago. His location was the Stockport area, so he's still local."

Leah nodded. "I'll give DCI Greco a ring shortly and tell him."

"When ballistics at the Duggan get back, hopefully we'll know something about the gun," Leah told them. "Speedy, did you get anything last night?"

"No, ma'am, something came up and I wasn't able to go. I'll go tonight," he said.

* * *

"Not hungry?" Grace asked sitting down opposite Greco at their table. "It all looks very nice and we don't know when we'll eat next."

"I've got a headache," he told her, stirring his coffee.

"So have I. It's called a hangover. But a full English should fix that."

"About what happened—"

"No, Stephen, not now. It really isn't a big deal. If it suits you, just forget all about it."

That was the problem. He couldn't forget. He'd slept with her, and broken his own rules. He didn't sleep with women he wasn't in a proper relationship with, but apart from that, Grace was a DC and he was her boss. The rules he'd broken there could see an end to his career. He watched Grace walk off to help herself to breakfast from the buffet. As she strode across the floor, a number of male eyes turned to watch her. She was wearing her long hair in a ponytail, but she'd done something to soften the effect. Scraping her hair back like that usually made her look hard, but not today. He watched as she went around the buffet, chatting to folk and choosing what to eat. She was completely unfazed by what had gone on between them. A fringe, that was the difference, he realised as she returned to their table with bacon and egg.

"You should get some, sort you out."

"Coffee is fine."

"Please don't sulk all day, Stephen. You make me feel as if it was all my fault, and it wasn't."

She was right. He wasn't handling this well. If he was honest, he was disappointed with himself. Not for sleeping with Grace, because he did like her. It was admitting it that was the problem. He couldn't shake the feeling that he was letting Suzy down in some major way, which was ridiculous when he analysed it.

"But it was your fault." He could have bitten his tongue off. He was still on the defensive. He couldn't help it. "You've done nothing but throw yourself at me for months." That had come out all wrong too. "Last night . . . that's not who I am. I don't do that sort of thing."

"Yes, you do, Stephen. Just admit it and move on. No one forced you. What is it you're worried about?"

"Any number of things. The job for a start. You work in my team. I'm your boss."

"I'm not going to tell anyone. Your reputation is safe with me, Stephen. I would never be so vindictive as to use what happened against you. Get this sorted inside that head of yours, because we have work to do."

Right on cue his mobile rang. It was Leah. They spoke for a few minutes as she brought him up to speed, then he checked the text Joel had sent him. "Rouse is alive and still in Manchester," he told Grace.

"So what now? Are we going home?"

"We'll have another word with Amani first."

Grace had cleaned her plate. "Does that mean we're checking out this morning?" she asked.

"Perhaps later today. We've got things to do here first. I've got a couple of phone calls to make."

"I'll get my coat and stuff while you finish your coffee."

He watched her walk off. She wasn't happy and he couldn't blame her. He needed to work out what was going on with his emotions, and fast.

Chapter 15

"She isn't here," a surly looking Marco told them. "Amani left last night. She didn't leave a forwarding address."

"Are you sure?" asked Greco. "She isn't hiding somewhere because she's afraid?"

"She was afraid alright. She reckoned you would tell the immigration people, and they would come for her. That they'd give her a hard time. Amani told me she'd had enough and was going."

"We wouldn't do that," Grace assured him. "We gave her our numbers. All she had to do was ring us. We would have put her mind at ease."

"You can't help her," he sneered. "Sooner or later the people who are doing this, bringing the boys into the country, would find her. They are killers. If they knew she had spoken to you, her life would be worthless. Amani had to get away before they came for her."

"Do you know who these people are, Marco?" asked Greco.

"No. I only know the man who organises things is English but not from round here. He speaks like her." He nodded at Grace.

"You mean he's from the North?"

"I don't know what he is. He spoke to Amani once on the phone. I answered it. They didn't talk for long but he terrified her. It was when Jamal first escaped from them."

The name Ray Shaw sprung to mind.

"We won't find her now." Greco said, once they were outside. He felt sure Amani would have gone back to London. "We need to look elsewhere for answers. Track Rouse down for a start."

"Back to Manchester, then."

"It looks like Rouse is in hiding. He's afraid of something or someone. That might make him more likely to talk to us."

"Perhaps this Northern man who frightened Amani?" Grace suggested.

"In the meantime we'll go back to the hotel. I've got to speak to a man from Border Control anyway."

"What about the local force?"

"They told me that during the season there are any number of foreign workers in the city. They haven't got the resources to check them all out."

"A feeble excuse. Sounds as if they're not even trying. Amani told us that Jamal had had medical tests. What do you reckon they were testing him for?" asked Grace.

"Could be anything. Maybe fitness for work like she said. There have been outbreaks of all sorts at that Calais camp."

"So where was this testing done, and by whom? Because I'm thinking it could be down to the Rashid Clinic."

"That's what Leah thinks too. Speedy is going back there this morning to sound them out. But that doesn't fit with the clinic's reputation. They carry out cosmetic procedures. They are high end and well known."

"I looked them up," said Grace. "They don't only do cosmetic stuff. Rashid and Horton are both top-notch surgeons. They were both surgeons in the NHS before they switched. We need to dig deeper. There will be something. Their name keeps cropping up. The event at the Millstone. I don't think that was a coincidence. I think Jamal went there to see someone, and before they threw him out he managed to eat some food. Whatever those doctors are up to, they will be getting paid for it with dodgy money. A lot of money."

Greco wasn't so sure. He'd researched the place, and it had an excellent reputation. Rashid was one of the best renal surgeons in the North West. He didn't have either of them down as people who needed to earn a fast buck by working for traffickers.

"It's possible the clinic is involved somewhere," he said to Grace. "But not in the way you reckon."

"I still think we should dig. Find a weakness, because there will be one."

* * *

Doctor Faisal Rashid peered through the window blinds at the car that had pulled up outside. It was that detective again, and this time he had a uniformed officer with him. What was going on? Jason must have said something at their last visit to bring them back. Or perhaps it was something he'd omitted to say. Jason Horton was fast becoming a liability.

Horton stuck his head around Faisal's office door. "Can you spare them a few minutes? It's nothing heavy. They're still asking questions about the event the other night, and that boy that was killed."

"They can't think the boy's death had anything to do with us, surely? Have you told them what we do here?" Faisal Rashid was angry. "We save lives, we do not take them. You must ensure these people understand."

Jason shook his head. "We have to be careful, Faisal. If we say too much, we could get into all sorts of trouble."

"You are talking in riddles. We have nothing to hide, so what could we say?"

Horton walked closer to his partner. "You do appreciate the good we do here, don't you? We can't stop now because of a little snooping by the police. We stay calm. We say only what we have to. Our work must continue, Faisal. Lives depend on it."

"We are a private clinic. We do what we are paid to do. If I'm put on the spot, Jason, I won't lie." Irritated at this interruption, Faisal Rashid followed his colleague down the corridor and into the reception area.

"This is most inconvenient. I have a tight schedule today. So please make this quick."

"We are investigating a murder," Speedy reminded him. "We are trying to piece together the dead boy's last movements. He was at the event your clinic held at the Millstone. Do you have any idea what he was doing there?"

"This again. Surely you have better information you can follow up?" He looked across at Horton. "The event was down to my colleague here. I wasn't involved. It was an introductory meeting for prospective clients. The clinic holds them periodically. There is nothing unusual in that."

"We believe that the boy was smuggled into this country from Calais. We have been told that he underwent medical tests."

Faisal Rashid shrugged. "Perhaps he did, but not here."

"We think it was." Speedy was chancing his arm.

"You are wrong. People who receive treatment of any kind here pay for it. It's a good thing that the boy was checked over. That place, the camp at Calais, is a cesspit. Anyone who gets out of there deserves all the help they can get. But I must emphasise again, they did not get it here."

"The boy, Jamal Ali, was deemed special enough to bring to Manchester, and not to work. Can you think why?"

Faisal looked at Jason Horton. "I can't begin to know that, Sergeant."

"What about you, Doctor Horton? Did he go to the Millstone to talk to you?"

"I didn't see the boy there," Horton insisted. "It is possible that he followed that hack, Rouse. He was at the event, uninvited and causing trouble. The boy will have seen the food on offer, and simply helped himself."

Speedy shook his head. "Rouse was tailing the boy, not the other way around. And that means that Jamal Ali had a reason to go to the Millstone, to seek you out."

"But not necessarily me. He could have wanted to speak to anyone there that night." Horton appeared to be mystified.

Faisal said, "Rouse is a troublemaker. We know he suspects the clinic of malpractice, but he has not been specific. He has been here a number of times. I don't know what he expects to find, but I do know he will be disappointed."

"Have you spoken to Rouse on any of his visits here?" asked Speedy.

"No, I left that to Jason."

Horton was silent for a moment. "He has it in his head that we are ripping people off. He thinks that our procedures are dubious and not worth the money. He plans to run an article in that paper of his, and expose us, try to encourage our customers to push for their money back. It's all rubbish. We do an excellent job, and I told him so, but he doesn't believe it."

Faisal coughed. "I'm sorry we can't help you further. I have a full list and must get on."

"Okay, but if Rouse comes back here, be sure to let me know." Speedy handed Horton his card.

Faisal Rashid was frowning as he watched the two policemen leave. "What exactly does that man Rouse have on us, Jason?"

"Nothing. He's chancing his arm."

Faisal studied his partner for a few moments. He was lying. He recognised the look, the body language. "If this is about your problem and Rouse prints his story, what then? Our reputation will be shot. We will get no more customers. Our clinic will be finished."

"I gamble a little, Faisal. As do thousands of others. It's not a sin. No one will be interested."

"You gamble at that club run by the villain, Shaw. Despite what you told the police, Rouse knows you from that damn club. Be very careful, Jason. Don't go getting drunk and talking to the wrong people."

"Rouse gets around. He knows people I know. Our paths have crossed, but I could hardly tell the coppers that, could I?"

"Does Rouse have anything on you?" Faisal's face was like thunder.

"He suspects I'm in debt, but he can't prove anything."

"And that thug, Shaw, where does he fit in to all this?"

Horton shrugged. "I have no idea. I don't socialise with the man."

Faisal wanted answers. "Is Rouse blackmailing you? As I told you, money has gone missing from the account. A lot of money, Jason, and consistently over the past few weeks."

"And I told you, that's down to a mix-up. I'll go and talk to our account manager at the bank. It will be fine."

Faisal didn't believe that for one minute.

"Hamid Khan, what are we doing about him?"

"I'm sorting that too."

"In what way are you sorting it? The man needs a kidney transplant. Are you simply going to snatch one out of thin air?"

"His brother agreed to be the live donor."

"Then why are we keeping the man waiting?"

Horton sighed. "Khan's brother has got cold feet, but I'm talking to him. He'll come round. I have described the procedure to him in detail, and explained that there is no danger to himself."

"Khan can't wait, Jason. He needs a new kidney. If his brother doesn't agree within the next twenty-four hours, we will have no choice but to transfer him to an NHS hospital. But there are waiting lists. His chances of a transplant will be greatly reduced. Have you told the family this?"

Horton nodded. "Another day, Faisal, and I'll talk the brother round."

* * *

While Greco made his phone calls, Grace did a little shopping around the Lanes. She wanted a gift for Holly and decided to get something for Matilda too. Greco was bound to forget, or even worse, not consider it important. She settled on two soft teddies in mugs with the girls' names printed on them — perfect.

Greco had said he'd be at least an hour on the calls and a Skype conversation with Leah Wells. He was all work. As she walked back along the seafront, Grace felt uneasy. Greco had not reacted to what had happened between them in the way she'd expected. For her it was no big deal. She liked the man. If he was up for it, she would consider a relationship, but he'd have to lose the attitude.

Grace stopped to buy a couple of sticks of rock. She was perusing the stuff on sale when she noticed him. He'd been in the other shops she'd wandered around too. The man was following her.

She felt her stomach tighten. He was a big man, swarthy and muscular. He'd positioned himself behind a display of postcards and each time he flicked it round he looked her way. Grace chose the rock and went to pay. She then spent the next few minutes fumbling in her bag. He was outside now, waiting on the pavement. This was her chance. Turning her back on him, she rang Greco on her mobile.

"I'm being followed," she hissed. "A brute of a man, I reckon he's been with me since I left the hotel."

"Where are you?"

"On the prom, outside the large red-brick hotel with all the flashing lights."

"Stay there, I'll only be a minute."

That was all very well, but once Greco arrived the man might do a runner. Grace wanted a photo. Someone from the local force or immigration might know him. She went outside and started to take pictures of the beach. Moving around slowly to include the pier, she just caught him. His head was down. The shot wouldn't be brilliant, but it was better than nothing.

"Give me the phone."

Grace froze. His hand was on her shoulder.

"Hand it over and I'll do you no harm."

There was no way she believed that. "No!" she said firmly, dropping it into her bag. He swore, then he pushed her forward, guiding her towards a number of cars parked across the road. His accent was foreign, possibly Eastern European.

"You are very foolish. You should have done as I asked."

"I'm police, and I'm not alone." She spoke as loud as she could, hoping someone nearby would come to her aid.

He laughed. "I know who you are, and why you are here. You are sticking your noses into something you do not understand."

They were perilously close to the black Volvo he was obviously heading for. If he got her inside that car, she was done for.

"Okay, you can have the phone." She reached into her bag and felt around. Her key ring was also a rape alarm. Trouble was, she had to find it. Her bag was like a bottomless pit.

His hand was around her upper arm. "Give me the bag. I don't have time to waste."

"Here it is," Grace said with a smile. She pulled the ring and bunch of keys from her bag and as she did so, pressed the button. Thankfully the battery was still good and the thing instantly emitted a high pitched, ear-splitting noise.

He swore again and pushed her to the ground. A few yards away, Greco was looking for her. Grace saw him and shouted. It took him only seconds to reach her side.

She picked herself up, gasping, "He's legged it! That way."

He helped her brush the dust from her clothes and picked up her bag from the pavement. "Are you okay? The place is crowded. Did you see where he went?"

"Up there somewhere. God, I was frightened. He wanted to get me into this car."

Greco was still holding onto Grace. "So he's on foot. Good. I'll call it in. The local force can take it from there."

Grace shook her head. "I'm fine. You can let go of me now."

"Sorry. I got a glimpse, that's all. But I saw him pushing you."

"I did get a photo of him."

Greco was already talking to the local CID.

"Text it to this number."

It took her only a few seconds to send the image to the local police. Greco continued his conversation. "They know him," he confirmed to Grace. "He's a Romanian long-distance lorry driver. They've been looking for him for a number of weeks. They'll get the car processed and send us a report asap."

"And he fits into this tangle of string where?" Grace was confused. The deeper they went into this case, the more complex it became.

"Jamal got a lift across Europe," he reminded her. "Perhaps that wasn't by chance."

"You mean that brute is one of the people who are bringing the lads into the country?"

"Could be. Hence his interest in you. He must know we've been to see Amani. I'm not surprised she left in such a hurry."

"What now?"

"The local force will take the car. Forensics will do their thing. We're going home." Greco put his arm around Grace's shoulder. "Enough excitement for one day, I think."

Grace winced. "I think my shoulder is bruised. That thug had strong hands."

Greco slipped his arm around her waist. "Sorry that had to happen. I should have been with you."

"I'm not a child, Stephen. We're working on a case. It comes with the territory."

"What did you buy?"

She smiled up at him. "A little something for the girls, and some rock. Holly and Matilda will love these. They've got their names on them."

Greco bent down and kissed her forehead. "I'm such a bloody fool at times."

"I won't argue with you on that one."

Chapter 16

Day 5

"Anything on Tony Rouse?" The question was met with blank looks and shaking heads. Greco sighed. He and Grace had arrived back late the night before. He'd come in early and updated the incident board with what they'd learned in Brighton. He'd also written a short report for them. The least Greco expected was for the team to meet him halfway.

"He's holed up somewhere, waiting for things to quieten down, bet my life on it," Speedy said eventually.

Greco's reply was terse. "That doesn't take an investigative mastermind to work out, given he's used his mobile locally recently. Joel, dig into his personal life. Is there anyone he might go to? A relative or friend?"

Greco looked at Speedy. "I'm surprised I have had to prompt you on that one. He's a reporter. Rouse is chasing a story he thinks is big. He isn't just going to abandon it. He'll be somewhere close. He'll want to keep an eye on what's going on. The chances are that someone is feeding him information."

"We could try the Crompton angle again, sir," Grace offered. "His wife has had a few days since her husband was killed. She might have remembered something. Who else Rouse worked with, for example."

Grace might have something.

"We'll go and talk to her shortly," Greco decided.

Joel looked up from his screen. "I had another look at that bus queue, sir. The blokes we saw were all wearing overalls. They're standard issue from Henshaw Bros."

"That's where Michelle works!" Speedy said.

"I went round there and spoke to them," Joel continued. "I showed them the image of the car, the one the Knifeman got into. The warehouse works around the clock. One of the shifts finishes at eleven, and one bloke remembers it. He knew the driver, and they acknowledged each other. He doesn't recall who got into the passenger seat, just that someone did."

"Go on then, don't keep us in suspense," Speedy joked. "Who was the driver?"

"Joe Tanner."

"The driver? Slicer's man?" Leah shook her head. "The lying . . ."

Greco looked at her. "He's hardly going to admit to anything, is he? Problem is, that by itself doesn't get us anywhere."

"It does confirm what my informant told me though, that the Knifeman was working for Shaw."

"Did this bloke see the car go into the multistorey?"

"Yes he did, sir."

"We should speak to Shaw again." Leah sounded annoyed.

Greco shook his head. "I doubt that will do any good. The man will swear he'd no idea what his driver was up to that night. We can't prove he put him up to it."

"That club of his. Tonight. And no excuses." Leah looked at Speedy.

Greco turned to Leah. "That isn't such a good idea. He's already seen both you and Speedy once this week. He'll be on his guard. I'll go. Grace, you can come with me." He saw her smile. She was at it again. In her book, this was a night out, another opportunity to get under his skin. "Speedy, go round to Henshaw Bros again. See if that bloke remembers anything else."

Leah Wells stood by the incident board, her arms folded. She looked angry. Was it because he'd side-lined her in favour of Grace?

"Why don't you look over the files again?" Greco suggested to her. "Look at what we've got so far, and see if we've missed anything. Try and figure out where we can get some answers. Get in touch with the Brighton police, see if they've got anything for us yet."

"I could come and talk to Crompton's wife with you," she suggested, glowering at Grace.

Greco shook his head and took her to one side. "You could have another word with that informant of yours. He might have something new to offer since you last spoke."

"Okay, but I can't guarantee anything."

"We'll have another briefing when I get back." He looked at Grace, who was putting on her coat. "We'll go and find Adam Crompton's wife. The hospital first and if she isn't there, her home."

* * *

A quick phone call confirmed that Crompton's wife had gone back to work, so Greco and Grace drove to the hospital.

"I'm surprised. She hasn't even had time to arrange the funeral yet."

"That's how some folk cope, Grace, by working through it. I would have done the same myself if McCabe had allowed it, but he wouldn't. He insisted I take the time off."

"They didn't have any kids, according to the information Joel gave me. Just him, her and a big house in Stalybridge."

"Which department does she work in?"

"Renal Care, under a Doctor Banister."

The two entered reception and asked for directions. They walked the three floors up.

"They look after the entire east side of Manchester here," Grace told him. "My Uncle Fred had dialysis here a couple of years back. What he really needed was a transplant, but that never happened."

"Shortage of donors?"

"Yes, but in the end Uncle Fred had a heart attack and died."

"Sorry."

"It's okay, we weren't close."

Molly Crompton was about fifty years old. She had short, curly dark hair that threw her pallor into sharp relief. She was thin, and looked tired, as though she hadn't slept for some time. As they approached, she turned and nodded towards an empty room off the corridor.

"They rang me from downstairs. You're police?"

Greco and Grace showed her their badges.

"Have you caught my husband's killer yet?"

"No, Mrs Crompton," Grace told her as they walked. "We think your husband's murder is linked to two others we're investigating. We were hoping you might be able to add something to the statement you gave our colleague."

"I told him everything I know. I've no idea what else I can tell you. Adam mixed with some odd types, Rouse for one, but murderers?" It was obvious that the idea had thrown her. "He must have got himself involved in something really shady this time. Adam had his nose in a lot of things. He didn't tell me much, but I reckon that Tony Rouse has a lot to answer for."

"Do you have any idea what they were working on?" asked Greco. "Anything you can tell us might help."

"I know that it was big. Rouse stood to make money from the story, so he'd promised Adam a generous fee. He was working all hours. Stayed out all night a week ago, staking out a private hospital in Chorlton."

"The Rashid Clinic?"

"Yes, but Rouse must have got it wrong. That clinic is one of the best. I told Adam so too. I've worked with Faisal Rashid and Jason Horton, and they are both excellent surgeons. I know that for a fact because I used to work for Jason Horton, here, in this very department before he left and Doctor Banister joined us. There is no way he'd be mixed up in anything unlawful. I told Adam to tell Rouse as much, and to stop wasting their time."

"Do you have any idea what he thought the clinic was up to?" Grace asked her.

"No, it could be anything. Perhaps something to do with the clientele. The Rashid Clinic carries out mostly cosmetic procedures these days. They have some very wealthy people queuing to get stuff done. Perhaps they'd heard a whisper about some celebrity or other."

"They do other things, apart from the cosmetic stuff, don't they?" Grace prompted.

"Nothing heavy. If people want to jump the queue they can pay privately and still see the same NHS doctor in an NHS hospital. Hospitals like the Rashid Clinic would not have the resources to carry out the procedures you could get done here for example. However they might specialise in something else other than plastics. Doctor Horton did work in urology, so he may offer certain procedures in that field. "

"Apart from your husband, did anyone else help Rouse with research?" asked Greco.

She thought for a moment. "Rouse has a girlfriend. Her name is Jean Smethurst. She used to work with the paper but took early retirement. She probably helped him."

"Do you know where she lives?"

"I've no idea. We did have dinner a couple of times, but always at a restaurant. He kept Jean very much in the background."

Then they heard a woman shouting from the end of the corridor. "Someone help us! My husband has collapsed!"

The woman was pushing a man in a wheelchair. He looked terrible — hunched over and barely conscious.

"Mr Khan!" Molly Crompton shouted, rushing to his side.

"Doctor Horton can't help us anymore. Everything has gone wrong. We've been left high and dry."

"He needs to see Doctor Banister right away." Molly Crompton called out to a porter. "Take Mr Khan to the dialysis ward!"

She turned to Greco and Grace. "I'm sorry, but I have to go."

"That man is in a bad way," Grace said, watching them enter the lift. "This is a renal unit. He must have kidney problems."

"So what was he doing looking to the Rashid Clinic for help?"

"I don't know, Stephen. If it's serious then a transplant is his best bet. The clinic is in no position to offer a procedure like that, so what were they trying to do for him?"

Greco looked back at the lift doors. "No one will discuss Mr Khan's illness with us — patient confidentiality. But we could talk to his wife. We'll give the Khans a little time, and then we'll do just that."

Grace nodded. "Is that what Rouse was investigating? Perhaps he thought the clinic was giving people false hope. You know, saying they could sort things when they couldn't and charging a fortune."

"A clinic like that could carry out a kidney transplant if they had a live donor, perhaps a close relative," Greco replied. "I've read that it isn't as complicated as it sounds.

If the donor is healthy, the outcome is usually good. We could do with knowing what Rashid thought he could do for that man."

"If that is what the Rashid Clinic is doing, they are keeping very quiet about it. I've seen nothing in their literature. It's all full of cosmetic procedures."

"Perhaps it's a rarity, a one-off," Greco added. "It's the only way they could do any transplants at all. The transplant programme is run by the NHS. The clinic would never be able to offer heart transplants for example, because they don't have access to the donor register. When we get back, check thoroughly and see what else they do offer, Grace." Greco checked his watch. "According to that map on the wall the dialysis ward is on the third floor. We'll have a cup of tea in the canteen then stroll up and see if Mrs Khan will talk to us. I wouldn't mind another word with Molly Crompton too."

Fifteen minutes later they arrived on the renal unit. Grace peeked through the glass window in one of the doors. Khan was alone in the room with his wife and hooked up to a machine. Greco knocked and smiled as Mrs Khan looked up.

"We're sorry to intrude," he began. "We're police officers investigating several murders. One of them is your nurse's husband. Would you mind talking to us for a few minutes?"

Mrs Khan shook her head, looking doubtful. "We know nothing about any murders."

"I'm curious about the Rashid Clinic. What did they offer to do for your husband?"

She hung her head. "We trusted Doctor Horton. Hamid should never have got this ill. We were promised that he would get better. It was going to cost every penny we had and what we could borrow from the family, but it would have been worth it."

"Did Doctor Horton explain how he hoped to make your husband better? What treatment did he have planned?" asked Grace.

"I thought he was a good man. I trusted that he wouldn't let us down." She wiped her eyes. "We have paid over most of the money and we are unlikely to get it back. We can't afford to go private again. If Hamid doesn't get a transplant, he will . . ." At that, she burst into tears.

"Did Doctor Horton offer your husband a transplant, Mrs Khan?" Greco asked bluntly.

"He is a good man. I know he meant well, but he raised our hopes and now we have been left like this."

"Who was going to be the donor?" Grace asked. "Did a close relative offer?"

"I trusted the doctors. They do wonderful work. They have saved many lives."

All very laudable, but she was deliberately ducking the question. Greco would have questioned her some more, but Hamid Khan started groaning. He was pale and clammy looking. His wife pressed the bell to summon a nurse.

"I must look after my husband. I can't tell you anything else."

Greco thanked her and left the room. Outside in the corridor, Grace was talking to Molly Crompton. "A sad case. The Rashid Clinic gave them hope."

"Mr Khan isn't up to being questioned right now," Molly told him firmly.

"I know that. I simply asked his wife about the treatment they'd hoped to get."

"I don't know what they were told. But I doubt they will have understood all of it. Doctor Rashid and his partner will have done their best but they can't work miracles."

"What about Horton? Mrs Khan speaks highly of him," Greco told her.

"I know his reputation but I haven't worked with him for a few years. If you want to know more, then go and ask them yourselves."

"Did Adam have a computer at home?" asked Grace, abruptly changing the subject.

"A laptop, yes. You are welcome to it, if you think it will help."

"It might. We think the killer took his notebook, so anything he'd stored on computer could be useful."

She smiled. "The notebook won't do him any good. Adam made his notes mostly in shorthand. But he did do a great deal of research for Rouse. His browser history might give you a clue."

"I'll send a PC round later," Greco told her.

"Did Adam never say anything about the Rashid Clinic?" Grace reiterated. "Not even in a casual conversation? You work in the medical profession. Didn't he ever ask you any questions, discuss anything he didn't understand with you?"

Molly Crompton thought for a moment. "Adam did want me to accompany him to an open evening at the clinic. It was about a month ago. Doctor Rashid was giving a talk about organ donation. He thought I would be interested, but I was working."

Grace frowned. "But the clinic is into cosmetic stuff."

"Yes, but Doctor Rashid tries to persuade all his clients to join the donor register. I don't think Doctor Horton was so keen. I've a feeling they don't get on that well anymore."

"Do you know why that is?"

"I'm not sure, but Horton is a risk-taker, Rashid is not." She thought for a moment. "Adam did tell me that Horton likes to gamble. That's something I've remembered. Adam spent several nights at some club in the city the week before he died. I got annoyed with him that night he stayed out all night, so he had to tell me what he was up to."

"Do you know which club?" asked Grace.

"No, but I'll go through his stuff if you like, see if I can find a card or something."

"Thank you, Mrs Crompton. The information you've given us could be useful."

Molly nodded and left them.

"Do you think Horton offered Hamid Khan a transplant?" Grace asked Greco.

"Without a donor, I don't see how he could."

"Perhaps they hoped to persuade a relative. I wonder how much money they've parted with."

"Whatever treatment he has had will have been expensive," Greco said. "We're unlikely to find out unless the Khans make a complaint and decide to tell us."

Chapter 17

"Brighton nick has been on the phone, sir. They've arrested the man who tried to abduct Grace." Joel Hough looked doubtful.

Grace sounded put out. "He was huge, built like a barn door and not very pleasant. If he'd succeeded, I wouldn't be standing here now."

"He's Romanian, one Cezar Todoran. He didn't say much, and no witnesses have come forward. The Brighton police had no choice but to let him go. Some fancy lawyer turned up and he got bail. They reckon they can do him for assaulting Grace, but unless we can come up with some sort of proof—"

"It is a serious matter. He could get away with it!" Grace folded her arms. "There were dozens of folk around, but no one will come forward. I even used my rape alarm for goodness sake! But still no witnesses. If it does go to court it'll be my word against his. Shame you can't run faster," she said to Greco.

"It was all over before I got there," he explained. "Too many people in the way for me to see anything."

Speedy smirked. "Stinks, doesn't it? You pressed your rape alarm?"

"Yes, I damn well did. The lump was about to bundle me into a car! What would my chances have been then?" She glowered at him.

Greco raised his voice above the chatter. "Any news on Rouse? Time is moving on. We need to wrap this up before we have another victim on our hands."

Joel shook his head.

Greco looked at him. "Find out all you can about a Jean Smethurst, Joel. She lives locally and is connected to Rouse. He may be staying with her. An address would be useful."

"It'd help if we knew what it was all about," Speedy added. "We're going around in circles but getting no nearer."

"I did as you suggested, sir," Leah told Greco. "But my informant hasn't heard anything else."

"Do we have someone watching Rouse's flat?" Greco asked.

"Yes," Joel confirmed. "And his mother's place on the Lansdowne. If he returns to either, we'll have him."

Grace looked doubtful. "It isn't Rouse who's killing people though, is it? That's who we need to find."

"Rouse knows why our victims were killed," Speedy reminded her. "A conversation with him could clear this up."

"That takes us back to the Rashid Clinic. That was what he was interested in."

Greco looked at the blank faces. "The clinic, Slicer Shaw, and young men being brought into the country from the Calais camp. What does that suggest to you?"

"Slave labour?" suggested Speedy. "Taken to the Rashid Clinic to get a clean bill of health. Perhaps one of the doctors is involved. That could be what Rouse had found out."

"It's a nice theory," Greco said, "But that's all it is. We need solid proof."

"I've made some enquiries, sir," Joel told them. "Within the last month a backstreet factory has sprung up in Openshaw, behind the takeaway on the High Street. I spoke to the manager, a Mr Hussain. He was very guarded, and wouldn't say where he got his labour from. Reckons he advertises in the local press but I've checked and I can't find anything."

"See if there is any link between the factory and the clinic. Go back, take Speedy and talk to the workforce. Find out what nationality they are and if they're being paid properly. If necessary bring the manager in. Perhaps an hour or so hanging around in an interview room will loosen his tongue."

"How are we playing it tonight, sir?" Grace asked, changing the subject.

"We'll be working, not playing," he said.

"I was thinking more about what to wear."

"Whatever you deem fit." Greco shrugged.

"The place is upmarket, sir," Speedy said. "It might belong to Slicer Shaw, but it brings in money and faces you'll recognise."

Greco saw Grace smile. She'd be done up to the nines, work or no work. "I'll pick you up at eight, so get off if you want." He looked at the clock. "I'll be right behind you."

* * *

Mickey was impatient. There had been no more calls from Slicer. Things were going too slow. He needed to strike again. Someone else close to Slicer had to die. He wanted in. He wanted it so bad he could think of little else. Phase one — Mickey wanted to run this patch for Costello. After that, who knew? Costello wouldn't live for ever.

Mickey picked up his personal mobile from off the table. His dark eyes flicked around the poky flat. He couldn't wait to be shot of the place. Money and power would do that. If his plan worked out he'd be able to live anywhere he liked. He scrolled through the contacts until he found his sister.

"Okay? Got anything for me?" he said to her.

"I asked the girls in the office but they weren't much help, Mickey. Susie said it was old-fashioned stuff no one used anymore."

"Well, the guy I'm after used it. Surely someone must know. Ask one of the older birds. See what they say."

"It won't get me into trouble will it, bro? That notebook's got a name inside it. The man that got himself murdered."

"It's fine. Stop stressing. Just doing a mate a favour, that's all. But I need to find out what the squiggles mean. You have to do this for me, sis. Get it right and there's a ton in it for you."

"Susie did copy some of it down and she showed it to her mum. She used to be a secretary to a solicitor years ago. She couldn't help much, but there was mention of a club in town. That posh place on Deansgate Locks."

"The Windfall?"

"Yeah, that one."

"Thanks, sis, I owe you one."

Slicer Shaw owned the Windfall. This was what he needed. Mickey couldn't settle. There was a long night ahead and he needed action. He went to his bedroom and rifled through his sparse wardrobe. He had a suit, the one he used to wear for work, but he hadn't worn the thing in months. It was dark grey, well-cut and stylish. Gran had gotten it for him when he'd left school. She'd wanted Mickey to get a job and get away from the Lansdowne. Some hope.

Half an hour later, the suit was sponged and brushed. Even better, it still looked good on him. Add a tie and a white shirt, and Mickey looked the business. His longish hair was combed back and gelled, and he was freshly shaved — no one would recognise him. More to the point, Slicer wouldn't.

* * *

Grace was wearing a short, clingy royal blue dress with a low neckline, set off with matching heels and a fur wrap. Her blonde hair was tucked into an elegant pleat. Heavier makeup than usual emphasised her dark eyes. She looked lovely. Greco couldn't help being impressed. In fact, as she stepped through the door of her house, Grace took his breath away.

"Cat got your tongue?" She grinned at him.

"You . . . you've done something." Stupid thing to say. Of course she'd done something. "You look wonderful. Perhaps a little . . ." She stopped him before he could say, 'over the top.'

"Quit while you're ahead, Stephen. But thanks for the compliment anyway. The place we're going to is popular with the wealthy young things that live in those swanky apartments on the Quays. They have money to burn. Who knows, some lonely footballer might come my way."

He bit his tongue. Any reminder that this was work would fall on deaf ears. Instead, he said, "I'm driving, but both of us should have soft drinks only."

"Spoilsport! What if a wealthy young thing wants to buy me champagne?"

"Refuse," was the sharp reply.

"I'm only joking, Stephen. I know what we have to do. How are we going to play this?"

"Gently. Neither of us are members, so if asked I'll have a discreet word with the doorman and tell him we're police."

"Are you expecting Slicer Shaw to be there?"

"I've no idea. The man maintains he's ill, so I'll be surprised if he is."

"Don't you find this just a tiny bit exciting? This club we're going to is the hottest thing to hit Manchester in a while."

"No I don't. I don't do clubs. I gave up staying out half the night in my twenties."

"Stephen Greco! You really are a first-class bore!"

He smiled. That's exactly what Suzy would have said.

"But you look bloody good in that snazzy suit. If I didn't know you'd give me the brush-off, I'd make a move on you right now."

He pulled into the car park at the rear of the Windfall. "Brighton not enough for you?"

She wagged her index finger at him. "Don't you dare, Greco! You know as well as I do what happened and why. You got drunk, we slept together, and the rest. Just proves you're human after all." She grinned.

They were approaching the entrance. "I'm trying to forget about it," he admitted. "It's not easy. We have to work together, and I am your DCI."

"What happened in Brighton was our business. The work thing is just a load of red tape. You might be a DCI but you're a man first, and men have needs. Even you, Stephen."

Chapter 18

Mickey got past the doorman, no trouble. He'd been busy arguing with a couple of blokes about the dress code, so Mickey had flashed him a smile and sidled by. Lax security, just what he needed. Once inside he made for the bar. The prices were steep. The club was a rip-off. He peeled a twenty from a roll in his pocket and ordered a beer. Time to take stock, see who was here. Mickey had done his homework. He knew all the main players currently connected to Slicer Shaw by sight. Sitting in the far corner was a doctor from some expensive private hospital. He and Slicer were said to have been pretty close recently. But would Slicer bother if he got killed? The woman he was with looked interesting. Mid-twenties, good shape, red hair and well dressed. She didn't let the good doctor out of her sight. Wherever he went, so did she. Someone else instead, then. Mickey wanted to keep it simple.

He drank his beer and scanned the room. There were a lot of people, all chattering away, and the place was noisy. The casino was off the main bar and entertainment area. He could see the tables were busy, with people spending money like it was water. There were a couple more doors off the main room. Mickey needed to know what was behind them.

Leaving his beer on the bar he walked across. No one took any notice of him. The first door was locked. The second led into a corridor, and then to the fire exit. He could hear the raised voices of two men arguing. One of them sounded foreign. A few feet along the corridor on the right-hand side, there was another door. The voices were coming from behind it.

"You should not have come here. You are a problem I can do without. How are you going to fill the order now?"

"Leave that to me."

Mickey didn't recognise either voice.

"I had to get away. What else was I supposed to do? The police arrested me. As for the order — that is no trouble. I can get hold of new candidates to fill it tomorrow."

"You will have to be discreet about it. We can't have you or them being seen going in and out of that place." Now Mickey recognised the voice. It belonged to Slicer.

"Give me the good doctor's mobile number. I'll ring him when I'm ready."

"No! He doesn't know you. I don't want him rattled. I will deal with him myself." Mickey leaned flat against the wall by the door and listened.

"I can be trusted."

"We'll see." That was Slicer again. "After that little setback, everything is back on track and I want it to stay that way. We stand to make a mint. What we don't need are complications. I want you to stay out of sight. You attract too much attention — the police for a start. They have been sniffing around again."

"Then deal with them. If the operation is to stay tight we can't afford loose ends. Speaking of which, how do we find that reporter?"

"He'll turn up," said Slicer. "He's mad for this story. He won't be able to stay away for long. When he does, I'll have him taken out."

Mickey had no idea what they were discussing. Slicer might trust him to kill when ordered to, but that was as far as it went. He retraced his steps back to the main room. The germ of an idea was beginning to take root in his brain.

* * *

Greco got the pair of them into the club by having that discreet word, and showing the doorman his badge.

Grace thought this was a mistake. "He'll go straight to whoever is in charge and before our feet touch, we'll be asked to leave."

"That's a little over the top. I told him we weren't here to cause trouble."

"Fat chance of him believing that!"

But Greco was looking around. "It's very pleasant in here." He was surprised. He hadn't expected to like it. But it was clean, with plush carpets and good quality décor and furnishings. Each table in the bar was surrounded by semi-circular sofas upholstered in deep red velvet. There wasn't a spilt drink or an empty glass anywhere. The lighting was subdued and relaxing. The barmen were smartly dressed and the music low-key. "Have you studied the faces on the incident board?" Greco asked Grace.

"Of course," she retorted.

"Look over there."

"The talented Doctor Horton. Wonder what he's doing here?"

"He gambles," he reminded her. "The club has a casino. Perhaps we should talk to him."

"No, Stephen, wait." Grace took hold of his arm. "That woman he's with, the one with the red hair." She paused while Greco shifted his gaze. "Do you know who that is?"

He shook his head.

Grace gave him a knowing smile. "That is Sadie Costello. And don't they look close. What do you imagine her and Horton are cooking up between them?"

"Costello as in . . . ?"

"Yes, she's Vinny's daughter. Twenty-six years old and the light of his life, if we are to believe all the intel."

"Could Horton be involved with Vinny Costello?"

"Who knows? But he's involved enough with his daughter. Look at the pair of them." The couple were now kissing.

Greco was trying to work out what this meant. How did it impinge on the case? "We need a word. At the very least Horton's presence here means he knows Shaw. Plus, it adds credence to the gossip about his gambling habit."

"Talk of the devil." Grace nodded at the man walking across the floor towards them. "Told you. So much for being infirm. Slicer looks fine to me. This is where we're quietly asked to leave."

Ray Shaw approached them, his smile soon falling away. "Can I help? I don't understand why you feel the need to come here. I spoke to friends of yours, and I told them all I know, which is nowt." A few seconds of silence followed. "Found out who shot my driver yet?"

Greco smiled at him and shook his head. "It's not that simple, Mr Shaw. Your driver was mixed up in another case we're investigating. A case that involves three murders, in fact. So for now, there's nothing I can tell you."

Shaw scoffed. "Tanner involved in murder? Most unlikely."

At that moment Jason Horton joined them. "Can I get you a drink, Ray? Why not come and join us?"

Slicer nodded at Greco and Grace. "These two are police. They're fishing for something. God knows what, because they won't find it here."

"Our colleagues spoke to you about the same matter," Greco explained. "The event at the Millstone and the young man we found murdered in the multistorey car park."

"Keep your voice down!" Shaw hissed angrily. "I will not have my guests upset by all this talk of murder."

"Look, come across to our table, have a drink. I'll happily answer your questions," Horton offered.

"Thank you," Greco said, graciously.

"Mingle," he whispered to Grace, leaving her behind and following Horton, Slicer at his heels.

Horton introduced Costello's daughter. "This is Sadie, a friend of mine. I'll get some drinks." Horton left them and went to the bar.

Greco smiled, taking the hand that was offered. "Nice to meet you. Interesting, finding you all here together like this."

Shaw's expression was sullen. "Don't go reading anything into that, copper. We're open to all. I don't pick and choose who uses my club."

Sadie Costello gave Greco a charming smile. "I must apologise for Mr Shaw. He's not very good at keeping his feelings under wraps."

"How about you, Miss Costello? Is that an art you've mastered?"

"Of course." She patted the seat beside her. "Sit next to me. Perhaps I can help clear things up. You're a policeman. I didn't need Ray to let that one slip. I have an instinct for such things. Honed over time." She smiled. "What are you investigating?"

"Murder, Miss Costello."

"Nasty business, murder. I don't envy you. But you can't believe that Jason is involved, surely? He'd never get up to anything so gross as killing people. He's a doctor, a surgeon. In case you didn't realise it, Mr Policeman, his remit is saving life, not taking it. He is a talented man and an excellent surgeon. Good to have in your corner should the need arise."

"Tell me more," Greco said, wondering what she meant.

"All that treatment he doles out at that clinic of his. Plastics is his forte, but people consult him for various reasons. My own father is a patient at the Rashid Clinic."

Greco smiled. "Your father is not well?"

"No, he's not. But he's doing fine. It won't be long before he's back on his feet."

Greco would have loved to ask exactly what was up with Vinny Costello, but he didn't. She was unlikely to give much away. "Very useful, having someone like Jason handy when there's a medical problem."

"Reassuring is what it is. Jason's skills are needed in this world. I don't like it when people belittle him. We are close. I know his weaknesses. This place for one." She nodded at the gambling tables.

"So why come here? Why not spend time in a club where there is no temptation?"

"That is not so easy, Mr Policeman. Jason is in debt. He owes Mr Shaw. Not a good place to be. I have offered to help but he has refused. We come here, Jason uses the tables, but he has a limit. If he wins, it helps pay his debt. Ray is fine with that. He does not exert any pressure."

He wouldn't dare. Greco could imagine how Vinny would react if Slicer Shaw leant on his daughter's latest squeeze.

Sadie Costello smiled again and shook her head. "Perhaps I've said too much. I shouldn't be discussing this with you. Speak to Jason if his gambling is relevant. But I should warn you, he is terribly embarrassed about the whole business."

Ray Shaw had been following their conversation. "You're discussing Jason? He's a damn good doctor and that's all there is to it."

"But flawed," Sadie added. "And I am trying to help him with that. But I don't think Mr Shaw is much bothered about it." She gave Slicer a poisonous look.

At that, Shaw turned and left them to join Horton at the bar. Within seconds the pair were deep in conversation. Greco wondered whether he was telling the good doctor that his girlfriend talked too much.

* * *

"Can I get you a drink?"

Grace gave the young man a smile and shook her head. "I'm okay, thanks. I'm working, so this fizzy water is fine."

"Have you been here before?"

Grace shook her head. "No, first time. You?"

"Same. That gives us something in common."

She hoped this wasn't some sort of chat-up line. Because if it was, he wasn't very good. "I doubt I'll be coming back. You?"

"Me neither. Not my scene. Too far out and very expensive."

"So why come at all?" Grace asked.

"I'm like you — nosey. I've got people to talk to. Facts to gather. You're police. You're not here by chance either. I heard the bloke you're with talking."

He was leaning against the bar, a beer in his hand. Grace put him at no more than twenty. He was tall and skinny but not bad-looking. He reminded her of someone but she couldn't think who. It was niggling her, on the tip of her tongue.

"What people and what facts?" she asked him.

"Nothing to do with you. Your best bet is to keep well out of it."

"Does it bother you? Me being police?"

He sniffed and took another swig of his beer. "Depends on how clever you are." He cocked his head to

132

one side, gave her a grin and walked off in the direction of the cloakrooms.

Weirdo! Grace looked around. Greco was deep in conversation with Sadie Costello. Horton was on the other side of the bar and Shaw had disappeared.

"All on your own?" Grace sidled up to Jason Horton. "Looks like my boss and your lady friend have hit it off."

"Best of luck to him, he'll need it. Sharp as a knife is Sadie."

Grace smiled. What did he mean by that? she wondered. "Have you met her father?" She was chancing her arm. He might not know about Costello, or if he did, he might not want to broadcast it.

He answered straight off. "Yes, and I've heard the hype. Not that I believe it, not any more. Vinny isn't a well man. He's practically confined to his home."

"He can still talk, though," Grace said. "Still issue orders, still get the job done, should the need arise."

"I don't like your tone, Detective. Mr Costello isn't the man he was. You lot have got him all wrong. You're looking in the wrong place."

Grace doubted that, but it did make her wonder if Costello was ill. Was that why Sadie was so into her hotshot doctor friend? "Where's your mate Slicer gone?" She scanned the room but he was nowhere to be seen.

"And do you have to refer to Ray by that name? In no way is it appropriate."

"Perhaps you don't know his history like we do," Grace retaliated.

"If what you say is true you would have him locked up by now."

Grace smiled back. "Not that easy. People are too scared to give evidence, you see. I'd like to know where he's disappeared to." She put her drink on the bar.

Horton smiled. "Weak bladder. An age thing." He turned away and went back to his table.

Grace checked her watch. She didn't want the villain slipping off without a chat. With a backwards glance towards Greco, who was still deep in conversation with Sadie, she made for the entrance and the cloakrooms. No one was taking much notice, so she ducked into the gents. Luckily it was empty.

"Mr Shaw!" she shouted. There was no reply. He'd obviously taken himself off to some quiet corner until she and Greco had left. Grace was wondering what questions he might be avoiding when something caught her eye. From under a door at the far end of the room there was a splatter of something on the floor. Stepping nearer for a closer look, Grace's fears were realised.

She darted forward and pushed the door open. It swung on its hinges to reveal another room containing half a dozen washbasins. On the floor, flat on his back in a spreading pool of blood, lay Slicer Shaw.

<h1>Chapter 19</h1>

Day 6

"I've got all the addresses and statements from last night's clientele. Not that they help much." Joel Hough shook his head. "Apart from Sadie Costello and Jason Horton, none of them are known to us."

Greco stood in the gent's cloakroom staring at the patch of dried blood. Bob Bowers, the pathologist, had arrived within an hour of Grace finding the body. Slicer Shaw was now on a slab at the Duggan. But how had it happened, and why? But more to the point, how come no one had seen or heard anything?

Grace walked into the gent's cloakroom and stood beside Greco. "I think that I might be the best witness we've got, sir. I've been thinking about this all night, running it over and over in my head. You were talking to Sadie, Slicer leaves you to it. I'm stood at the bar talking to some weirdo. I think that weirdo was our man. I think he was watching Slicer and chatting to me as a cover. He saw Slicer go towards the gents, gave me the brush-off and followed him in here."

"Ray Shaw was shot. One bullet to the chest. The Duggan will confirm if the bullet came from the same gun that killed Joe Tanner."

"Are you listening to what I'm saying? I think I spoke to him. I was as close to him as I am to you," Grace said with feeling. "I just thought he was a bit odd. It never occurred to me that he was up to something."

Greco turned to look at her. "You can't be sure though, can you, Grace? The fact of the matter is that anyone here last night could have killed Shaw."

"No, it was my weirdo. I know it was. I know it in my gut. Not something you go in for, but I do. The more I think about the comments he made, and his attitude, the more certain I am."

"In that case, help Joel pin him down on the CCTV footage he's about to start wading through."

"Where is the camera, sir?"

"At the entrance. So if he was in here, then we have him recorded."

"Did you get anything from Horton and the others?" she asked him.

"Horton, no, and all Sadie Costello wanted to talk about was the good doctor's gambling habit. I got the impression she was using that to stop me asking about other matters. Problem is, I don't know what those other matters were."

"Did you not ask her?"

"We were interrupted. Then you found the body and that was that."

"I had a chat with Horton about Sadie. Just my instinct twitching again, but I got the impression he was wary of her."

"I think our Miss Costello is smarter than she pretends. She orchestrated that conversation. She was making me think she was revealing stuff, when all the time she was steering the conversation."

"Well, at least we know who didn't shoot Slicer. It couldn't have been Horton or Sadie. The pair of them have you and me as alibis."

* * *

The team were assembled in the incident room. Greco was updating the board while relaying to McCabe what had happened. The rest of them sat quietly, waiting.

"Ray Shaw's death leaves a huge hole in Costello's operation," Greco began. "He'll want to fill it fast. It's important that we find out who did it. But equally important is why. Is this a takeover bid, or something else?"

"There have been no whispers, sir," Leah added. "The streets have been quiet. No one is talking. I'll see what the latest event has thrown up later. But from what I know already, I bet this is as much a mystery to the villains as it is to us."

"There is another aspect we haven't considered," Greco said. "Perhaps it is Costello himself who wanted rid of Shaw. There have been rumours." He looked at Leah, who nodded.

The team fell silent, considering this.

Eventually Speedy said, "Slicer has run things smoothly around here for years. Why rock the boat?"

"Villains do fall out," Greco reminded him.

"I think we're looking at someone entirely new. An unknown face, who has been watching and worked out a strategy for a takeover," Grace suggested.

"That would take some guts!" Leah exclaimed. "If Costello got hold of him . . ." She shuddered. "Well, I wouldn't want to be in his shoes."

"I put the theory forward because of someone I met at the club last night," Grace explained. "An odd young man who I now think was playing games with me. He was certainly using me to pass the time while he kept an eye on Slicer. He knew I was police, even made a point of

137

commenting on it. I think we should at least find out who he is and speak to him."

"You're looking at the CCTV footage. You'll pin him down soon enough. Leah, your informant may have heard something by now. There may be nothing on the streets about a takeover, but theories about Slicer's death will be circulating. I want to know what is being said.

"And you, Stephen?" McCabe asked.

"I want to speak to Jason Horton. I want to know more about what he does at that clinic of his. I'd also like to know how he met Sadie Costello. She isn't a woman you meet by chance." He looked at Leah. "You might ask your informant if he knows anything about Rouse's whereabouts while you're at it."

"I can come with you," McCabe suggested.

"It's okay, sir, I'll take PC Dobbs with me."

The last thing Greco wanted was the super trying to take over. He was a good copper and all right in small doses, but Greco didn't want to work in his shadow.

He turned to Gareth Dobbs. "You can drive. I'll see you in the car park."

Greco went to his office and re-read the file on the Rashid Clinic. There wasn't much, certainly no mention of Horton doing anything that he didn't charge top dollar for. If it came to it, he might have to interview Sadie Costello again too. How would that go down with her father?

* * *

Jason Horton greeted them. "Dreadful business. I presume you're here about last night. Sadie was very upset. She's known Ray since she was a child." That conjured up an interesting image in Greco's head. The small child, sitting on her father's knee while the mobsters discussed their latest plans.

Horton led them into a small anteroom off the main entrance. "Make yourselves comfortable. I'll organise some coffee."

"There's no need," Greco assured him. "This shouldn't take long."

"I didn't see anything last night," Horton began. "You were sitting only a few yards away from me, talking to Sadie when it happened."

"We have to speak to everyone who was there," Greco told him. "Neither you nor Miss Costello are suspects. I know that both of you were talking to me and my colleague at the time. However, you may have noticed something odd, heard something. At this point we need all the help we can get."

"Wish I could help you, but I'm afraid I can't. Nothing out of the ordinary comes to mind. It was a fairly typical night at the club. Except for poor Ray of course."

"You and Miss Costello are there often?"

Horton shrugged.

"Does her father ever go with you?"

"Vinny isn't up to it, I'm afraid. Anyway, it's not his thing — clubs, casinos, staying out late. He's very much a pipe-and-slippers man these days."

Greco was struggling to get his head around the idea of Vinny Costello with a pipe and slippers. "You've treated him here, I believe?"

"You know I can't discuss my patients. You would have to ask him."

"I presume he didn't want plastic surgery?"

"Look, DCI Greco, you can presume all you like, but I will not discuss my patients' health. However, I will say that plastic surgery isn't the only procedure we do here. We offer medical consultations and other types of surgery too."

"But that's where the money is, isn't it? In plastics," Greco continued.

"Yes, and it forms the major part of what we do."

"You certainly have a fan in Miss Costello. She couldn't sing your praises loud enough."

"She prattles on."

"Hamid Khan was a patient of yours. He and his wife believed you could help him. Why was that, when what he needs is a kidney transplant?"

"Like I just said, I can't discuss my patients with you."

"He is currently languishing in Manchester General on dialysis. His wife thought you were going to make him well. How did you plan to do that?"

"We were hoping to get a live donor, a close relative." Horton sounded impatient. "It is permissible for us to carry out the procedure in such circumstances. I am a renal surgeon with many years' experience in the NHS behind me. Five years ago, I re-trained in plastics. A very lucrative add-on," he smiled.

Greco decided to change the subject. "Where did you meet Sadie Costello?"

Horton smiled. "Here, at the clinic. Sadie came to us for treatment."

"Cosmetic treatment?"

"I can't say."

Greco waved a hand. "Yes, of course — patient confidentiality. I will be speaking to her. Offer her the opportunity to expand on what we spoke about last night."

"That is your prerogative, but I should tell you that Sadie has gone to stay with her parents for a while. I have no idea when she'll be back."

Great! That meant any contact would inevitably go through Costello's people. Sadie would be well coached in what to say long before he could get a statement.

"Do you have any idea why anyone would want to kill Ray Shaw?"

"I've no idea. He was a charming man."

"That depended on how you knew him, Doctor. Believe me, Shaw could be far from charming when he chose. Given that you owed him money, you must have known that."

"That is my private business. I refuse to discuss it here."

"If you didn't have my colleague as an alibi, that fact alone would have given you a motive. How much do you owe, Doctor Horton?"

"None of your bloody business. And it has nothing to do with the case you are investigating."

They were going round in circles. Horton wasn't going to tell them anything useful.

Faisal Rashid stormed in without knocking.

"You again! Don't you have better things to do? There was another murder last night. You can't possibly think it has anything to do with us. I can't understand why you insist on rushing here whenever there is any criminal activity in this town."

Greco smiled at him. "I can assure you that this is just routine. We have to speak to everyone who was in the club last night."

"And that includes you, does it, Jason? I should have known. We spoke. I thought you were giving that place a wide berth."

"Sadie and I were having a few drinks, Faisal, that's all."

Greco looked at Horton. "Am I to presume that you couldn't find a close relative to be a donor for Mr Khan?"

The question had been directed at his partner, but Rashid responded, his face blank. "What are you talking about?"

"Hamid Khan needs a kidney transplant. Doctor Horton here was supposed to help him."

Faisal Rashid's dark eyes narrowed to pinpricks. "We do not have a transplant programme here, or anything like one. It's a nice idea but it would not work in practice. Transplants need donors, don't they? And there is the problem." He turned to look at his partner. "We will speak later. Why are you discussing our business with all and sundry, Jason?"

"We are not all and sundry as you put it, Doctor Rashid. We are the police. Currently we have four murders on our hands. So I will ask any questions I think fit, and expect answers."

Faisal Rashid marched out of the room.

"He doesn't see things as I do," Horton said. "Had a relative come forward, I would have done the operation for Hamid Khan. Faisal frowns on us doing anything other than the plastics stuff. It's where the money is, you see."

Greco didn't think Rashid knew anything of interest anyway. Horton was the one with answers. The problem was getting them. While he continued to hide behind patient confidentiality, it was doubtful they would get anywhere. Greco decided to leave it — for now.

Chapter 20

Mickey paced the floor of his small flat. Adrenaline had kept him awake most of the night. His head ached from thinking about what he'd done. Killing Slicer was all very well, but where exactly did it leave him? He'd destroyed his only contact with Costello.

Stupid! Stupid fool! You should think before you dive in. Too bloody handy with weapons, always have been. What now? How do you get what you want if no one knows you're around?

Mickey had collared Slicer in the gent's toilet. He'd told the villain that he wanted in. He said he'd overheard him and knew that there was a lot of money in the pipeline. He wanted his share. Mickey wanted a part in whatever operation Slicer was planning. The man had laughed at him — called him a stupid kid, shook his head and told Mickey to mind his own business. He was to come when called, and until then to go away and not make waves. Mickey had got angry. He wasn't going to be treated like a piece of dirt. As Slicer had stood there laughing at him, Mickey had shot him dead.

He could contact Costello direct. Tell the big man he was ready for work. Mickey rubbed his eyes and screamed with rage. Costello would think he was a fool. He'd be dead in a gutter before the day was out. He'd planned to take over, run this patch for himself, but he had nothing. No money, no contacts, no access to the drugs he'd need to sell on. And there was more to it than just running drugs. Slicer had been into other stuff. Problem was, Mickey hadn't let him live long enough to find out more.

He rang his sister. "Need your help," he hissed down the phone. "I've ballsed up. I need to find out what the cops know about those murders. The youngsters and Slicer Shaw." She didn't reply straight off. She'd be thinking it through. "You can get hold of stuff. I need this. Come on, sis, you're in the right place."

"That boy in the multistorey was an illegal. Probably brought here to work in some backstreet sweatshop. The bloke in the pub worked with that reporter, Rouse. That's all I know." She hung up.

So Slicer had been mixed up in people trafficking. Mickey kicked out in fury, hitting the fridge and denting the door. He'd had no idea. He didn't know the first thing about how to make it happen for himself.

* * *

"I've been glued to this screen for an hour or more. Where the bloody hell is he?" Grace was beginning to think she'd dreamed him up.

Joel was unsympathetic. "Not much fun, is it, the CCTV work? You shouldn't have been so keen to say you knew what he looked like. You'll know better in future."

She ignored him. "The time stamp says nine thirty. Greco and I arrived at nine."

"Was he already there?"

"I don't know. He might have been. He stood at the bar, drinking. When I spoke to him we'd been in there about ten minutes or so."

Joel flicked the footage back to nine o'clock. "Sit down, get comfy and watch the main entrance. It was very busy around that time."

"There's me and Greco," she pointed out. "Go back a little further."

Joel pointed to some people at the door. "Bit of bother there. Even in an upmarket place like the Windfall."

"It's the way that pair are dressed. They were never going to get in wearing jeans and T-shirts."

It was easy for the eye to be distracted. The altercation between the two blokes and the doorman had taken their attention.

"Look!" Joel froze the film. "Sneaking in around that lump of a bouncer. Is that him?"

He was tall, wearing a suit and white shirt. He had his hands in his pockets and slunk past the doorman with no bother. "Joel, you're a star! Yes, it is." Grace leaned forward and stared at the screen. "And we've got a good, clear look at his face. Print me a copy, please."

With the image in her hand, Grace went to find Greco. "This is my weirdo," she announced, placing it in front of him. "I reckon this is the bloke who shot Slicer."

Greco studied the printout. "He's young."

"And he's tall and skinny. Fits his description too." Grace nodded at the board in the other room.

"Are you saying that this individual could be responsible for the murder of the two boys as well?"

"Why not?"

"Because it's a leap too far. I can't see where killing a couple of trafficked runaways could be connected with the murder of Tanner and Shaw. Besides, the method was different."

"That could be deliberate. Keep an open mind, that's all I'm saying. Another thing, does he look familiar to you?"

She waited while Greco studied the image. Finally he shook his head. "No. Sorry, I don't know him."

"I'll stick it on the board."

"We need his identity. He was at the club so we'll have to speak to him in any case."

"Joel is busy fitting names to faces from the CCTV as we speak." She paused for a moment. "What's the betting he can't pin a name on my weirdo?"

* * *

"You the 'kid?'"

The voice was deep, thick and foreign. Mickey felt a chill in his bones. The call had come through from Slicer's mobile. "Who wants to know?"

"Meet me, we need to talk. Things are different now. Slicer is dead. Plans have to change."

Mickey smiled to himself. He'd worried for nothing. This was his way back in. "Where?"

"Know the old mill on Cotton Street, at the back of the DIY store?"

"When?"

"Now. I'll give you ten minutes. Ground floor. I'll be waiting."

Mickey put his blade in the inside pocket of his hoodie. Despite his relief at the contact, he was walking into the unknown. He'd no idea who this stranger was, but it was likely he was the foreign bloke Slicer had been talking to at the club.

Leaving Atlas House, he walked across the square, and headed for a path leading to the rendezvous. Cotton Street was only a five minute walk away. Problem was, nothing happened there anymore. When the mill had been active it had bustled with workers. Even when cotton was long gone the mill had been divided up into units, each housing a small business. Now it was lying empty and derelict, yet another red-brick hulk on the skyline.

Mickey crept inside a gap in the ramshackle double doors and shouted into the gloom. "Hello!"

"Quiet, kid! I'm over here."

He walked towards the voice. The man stood behind a pile of old wooden pallets. He was tall, thickset, with a shaved head and heavily tattooed arms. Mickey shuddered. He'd have to watch his step. Anger this one and he'd end up worst off.

"Slicer bought it last night. Some scrote put a bullet in his chest. Problem is, he had information that I need if I'm to carry on the good work." The man smiled, showing a mouthful of gold fillings. "That is where you come in, kid. You worked with Slicer. I want to know everything he told you."

Mickey shrugged and backed off a few feet. "He told me nowt. I did the job, took my money, end of story. I didn't even know why the poor bastards had to die."

"You're lying." Mickey could see the anger on his face. "I don't have time for this. Slicer or that driver of his must have spoken to you. Tanner had a slack mouth." He stared at Mickey through dark slits of eyes. "I don't want to hurt you, kid, but I will if you won't talk to me."

Mickey was ready to run. The adrenaline was pumping. This one was dangerous. "Told you, can't help." He turned and made for the door as fast as his legs would take him. The stranger was heavy, he'd not catch him. Mickey could outrun the best.

His arm was extended ready to push what was left of the door out of the way. A searing pain in his back floored him. He hit the concrete with a crash. The bastard had thrown something heavy and it had caught him between the shoulder blades. Turning his head, Mickey saw a thick metal bar lying at his side. He could do nothing to help himself, the breath had been knocked from his body.

Grabbing him by the legs, Cezar Todoran dragged Mickey back to the pallets. Mickey was frantic. He kicked out wildly, hitting the man on the shin with the toe of his shoe. Todoran snarled with rage. Hauling him up onto a pallet, he laid Mickey down on his back. "You will talk to me, you thin streak of piss, or you will die."

Mickey was shaking. He had to think, and fast. He had to get away before this headcase did him some real damage. "Slicer never told me anything!" he yelled. Sweat was pouring off him.

"Then you will suffer."

Todoran began strapping him down with a length of rope. Mickey tried to struggle free but he was no match for the big man. He screamed into the empty mill in the vain hope that someone would hear. The man had hold of his wrist, pressing his hand down flat so that his fingers were splayed against the wooden slats of the pallet.

"Speak to me now. You are running out of time."

"Slicer didn't trust me. He never talked about what was going on. I hadn't known him that long."

"You are not trying hard enough."

"No!"

Mickey had seen what was in the man's hand. Seconds later the lump hammer hit, crushing the knuckle of his middle finger.

"Speak!" Todoran ordered. "The doctor, what is his name?"

Mickey groaned. He was going to pass out. "I . . . I don't know any doctor."

There was a moment of silence.

"I have little patience and even less time. You must know something." Todoran raised the hammer again and brought it crashing down, this time on the other hand.

Mickey shrieked and fainted, but a bucket of cold water thrown over him brought him back to consciousness. He screamed again. He couldn't feel his hands.

"I think the doctor was called Horton. He works at a clinic in Chorlton. He was at that club Slicer owns. They talked a lot. I looked him up. I don't know anything else," he panted. He could feel his heart racing. "I've told you all I can. Let me go, please. I won't say anything."

"That is right, you won't." Todoran patted his arm and smiled down at him. "You should have told me what you knew at the start. I could have made this easier for you."

"Please . . . let me go."

Todoran shook his head. "Sorry, you are out of luck."

He fitted a silencer onto a pistol, and held it to Mickey's temple.

"Bye, kid," he said, and pressed the trigger.

* * *

Todoran stepped back from the blood pooling on the floor by his feet. The kid had had to die. He could identify him. Now he would find this doctor and make him pay the money Shaw owed him. Todoran was angry. Shaw had been tight-lipped about the operation. Never used names, and never discussed plans. Just issued orders and handed over what was owed. He looked at the lad. He'd been good with a knife according to Slicer. Shame. If he'd been forthcoming a bit sooner, Todoran could have used him.

Todoran had found Shaw's body last night only minutes after he'd been shot. He'd searched it and taken the mobile phone. Not that it had been much use. The only number on it had belonged to the kid.

He'd left his vehicle at a service station nearby. Time to retrieve it and find this clinic. If the good doctor valued his life, he would cooperate. He'd pay over the money Todoran was owed. He'd also tell him what he was to do with the two dozen or so refugees he had hidden inside his truck.

Chapter 21

It had been raining since daybreak, a fine drizzle. The wet, grey mist hanging over the estate made it look even bleaker than usual. DI Leah Wells parked up and made for the Grapes pub. It was nearly lunchtime, so Roman would be in his usual seat. She hoped he could help. The Duggan had contacted Greco earlier. The bullet that killed Slicer had been fired from the same gun that had shot his driver, Tanner. Leah had left the team discussing what that might mean. Speedy had taken it as proof that Costello was clearing the decks, but Leah couldn't see it. Why would he? His operation in this part of Manchester was working like a dream.

As she entered the pub, Leah was greeted by a chorus of wolf whistles from the men stood around the bar. It didn't matter, none of them knew her.

"Leave the girl alone!" Roman McLaughlin shouted to them. "Sit over here, doll, I'll get you a drink."

"Coke will do, Roman." She smiled at him.

"Want something to eat?"

Leah shook her head. There was no way she was eating anything prepared in this place.

Roman sat down opposite her. "Slicer? Heard this morning. Bad business. It's got Costello's people shook up."

"One of my colleagues did wonder, like you said last time, if the big man wanted rid."

"Could be, but last night wasn't down to Costello, not with his daughter on the premises. There is a whisper that Vinny is not so good. Word has it that he's spending a fortune on private healthcare. For the time being at least, he'll want things to remain stable."

That could be the reason Sadie was seeing Horton. She wanted treatment for her father. "Do you think this is someone new? Someone who knows the score with Vinny and is looking to take over?"

"Could be, pretty lady, but no one is talking."

"Are you sure, Roman? Not even a whisper? Anything, no matter how small it is. We really need to break this before it escalates."

He nodded. "One piece of info I can give you is that Slicer had a visitor last night. A Romanian bloke called Todoran. He is on the run from the police down south. Nothing he couldn't wriggle out of, but he chose not to hang around. A source told me he was at Slicer's club last night. He could be who you're looking for."

Leah knew it could not have been him. The gun was the one used to kill Tanner, and as far as they knew Todoran wasn't around when Tanner had been shot.

"We don't think he was the killer."

"Believe me, he's your best bet. What type of gun was used?"

Leah thought for moment before replying. She was reluctant to give out information. But if she said nothing, she'd get nothing back.

"A Glock," she told him.

"In that case, I do have something. Within the last few days someone sold a Glock to a youngster from the Lansdowne."

"Who sold the gun, Roman?"

He smiled. "You know better than to ask that. And he didn't get the kid's name either."

"Did this kid say anything to the seller?"

"No, but the seller was surprised. He reckoned the kid's weapon of choice was a blade."

Leah turned this over. Could this be their knifeman? She saw the look on Roman's face.

"You work it out."

"We will, eventually, but why the change of weapon?"

"You have to get close to knife someone. If you want keep a little distance, then a gun is your best bet."

The two sets of killings were very different. Two lads, running away from God knows what, and two local villains. If this was down to the same killer, it was possible that this was a deliberate ploy to throw the police off the scent.

"He did tell me something that might help you. The kid has a twin sister. She's not like him. She's legit and working."

"Any word on Rouse?"

Roman considered this then shook his head. "Gone to ground, and who can blame him? Costello will have got wind by now. The poor sod will be a target."

* * *

Grace had had enough. She looked at Joel. "I need a break from this. That factory in Openshaw, let's give that a whirl instead."

Joel Hough looked doubtful. "Sure the boss will go for it? He wants these faces looking at urgently."

"It's a waste of time. There won't be one we recognise. He did ask you to go back and speak to the manager again. I'll have a word." Grace left Joel and went to find Greco. He was in his office, files in hand.

She smiled at him. "Me and Joel are going to take an hour. We'll check out that factory. See what we can turn up. We've been through most of the CCTV from the club last night but no one sticks out. To be honest, I'm going face blind. They are all unknowns, mostly twenty-somethings from the posh part of town. There's no one that looks remotely dodgy."

"Neither does Sadie Costello, and look who her father is. Okay, but don't go getting into bother," he warned.

Grace beckoned to Joel, grabbed her stuff and they were off. "You can drive. I've no idea where the place is."

"It's near those old buildings they're pulling down by the canal."

"What are they still doing there? Everything in that area was condemned months ago."

"Not this one, apparently. Hussain Textiles has been there for over a year. They'll know their days are numbered. When the axe falls, they'll soon pack up and move somewhere else."

"The building can't be safe. Most of the properties are old warehouses. Very few of them have their roofs still intact."

"They're cheap and that's all that counts. These outfits cut costs to the bone. Profit is everything."

They drove down Ashton Old Road, across the railway, and turned right into a backstreet. Joel drove for about half a mile past row upon row of red-brick terraced houses, punctuated by corner shops and the odd pub. When the road ended at the canal, they saw the large, crumbling building.

"Keep your eyes open. They aren't expecting us. We don't have a warrant so we'll have to keep it low-key," Grace told Joel.

They walked into the building. The single desk in the reception area was covered in paperwork and dirty mugs. Stacks of used cardboard boxes and packaging littered the floor.

Most of the boxes were empty. Grace moved a couple out of the way to get to the desk. "Health and Safety would have a field day in here."

"What d'you reckon? Anyone working, or what?"

"There'll be poor souls working alright. Round the clock, if the rumours are right," Grace replied. Off the reception was a long, narrow corridor with yet more boxes blocking the passage. "Let's find out."

They were a couple of metres in when a man clad in an overall appeared from behind a door at the end. He waved his arms at them.

"Mr Hussain is out. Come back later."

Not much of a welcome, but Grace smiled nonetheless. "Is there someone else we can speak to?" They waited while he wrestled with this. Had he even understood them?

"I'm DC Harper and this is DC Hough. We were hoping Mr Hussain could help us with a case we're investigating."

"He knows nothing. He's out. There is no one here who can help you."

Grace was about to argue the point with him when a teenage lad stuck his head around the door. There was a heated exchange in a language neither detective understood, then the lad disappeared again.

"One of your staff?" Grace asked, peering after him. The boy looked grimy. His clothes had seen better days. He was thin, and his dark hair badly needed cutting

"No, he's on placement from a local school," the man explained.

Grace gave him a doubtful look. In her opinion, there was no way that lad had come from any school, local or not.

"Could we have a word with him, please?"

"Why? He's just a boy. What use can he be to you?"

"A quick word, that's all," Grace insisted.

The man's eyes narrowed. He muttered something unintelligible and disappeared into the corridor. Moments later he reappeared with a different youth, who was definitely not the lad Grace and Joel had just seen. This one was far tidier, and wore a shirt and tie and smart pants.

Grace folded her arms. "That isn't him. The boy who was just in here was small, poorly dressed and very young. Too young to be working here full-time."

"He is not working. I told you. He is here on work experience, from his school."

"Can I have the details? His name, the school and any work records you have for him."

"Everything is in the office. It is locked. Only Mr Hussain has the key and he is not here. You will have to come back much later." He opened the main door. "You must leave now."

"Is there anyone here who speaks reasonable English? We simply want to clear a few things up," Grace said.

"Speak to Mr Hussain later. No one here can help." He closed the main entrance door behind them, and Grace heard the key turn in the lock.

"What d'you make of that?" she asked Joel.

"Something to hide, obviously. What do we do now?"

"Back to the nick. I'll speak to Greco, see what we can do. But one thing's for certain, we will be coming back."

* * *

"Crompton's laptop is being looked at by the IT boys at the Duggan," Speedy told Greco. "They'll make it quick and get back."

Greco was studying the notes Leah Wells had given him about her meeting with Roman McLaughlin. "The Knifeman has a twin sister. That must narrow things down, surely? How many twins are there on the Lansdowne?"

"Are we even sure that's where he's from? And if he is, does his twin live there too?" Speedy shrugged. "Not sure that little snippet helps on its own."

Greco left his office and walked to the incident board, where he transferred the notes for the benefit of the team.

Speedy nodded at the photo of Grace's weirdo. "Who's that?"

"He was at the club last night. Spent some time talking to Grace. She reckons it was deliberate, and that his real purpose was keeping an eye on Slicer."

"I know him."

Greco wasn't surprised. Speedy knew a lot of people around here. "So is he a weirdo, like Grace seems to think?"

"I don't *know* him exactly but I know who he is. Michelle, my girlfriend, he's her brother. She moved into mine recently and she brought along a photo of them both."

Greco stared at his sergeant for a moment. "Are they twins?"

Speedy brushed his hair back from his face. "I'm not sure, but I'll soon find out."

He went out into the corridor, where he spent the next few minutes on his mobile.

"They are twins, sir. He's Michael Dent, commonly known as Mickey. He lives in one of the tower blocks, Atlas House."

Greco tapped the board. "This information has come from a good source, Leah's informant. This, coupled with Grace's gut feeling, could mean we've finally got something. We'll go and have a chat."

"Michelle says he's a layabout, doesn't work. So he should be in."

* * *

They made their way down to the car park, where Greco handed Speedy the keys. It took less than ten minutes to reach the estate. Mickey Dent lived on the fifth floor and the two detectives took the stairs.

"It's okay for you. You're a fitness freak," Speedy puffed, struggling to keep up with Greco.

Greco smiled. "Not recently. Simply not had the time."

"You're still in better shape than me."

"You know what to do. When this is over, come running with me."

"Running? You're having a laugh! I'm not that keen."

They walked along the fifth floor deck to number twelve. The flat, like so many others in this godforsaken place, looked unlived in.

"This is the one. Tattered curtains, peeling paint on the door . . ." Greco knocked. The seconds ticked by. He banged harder.

"He's either not here or he's hiding. What d'you think? Dare we go inside?" Speedy asked.

"We've no warrant," Greco reminded him.

"One kick, that's all it would take." Speedy peered through the grime-streaked window, and pointed at something. "Does that shape look like a body to you, sir?"

"I can't see any shape."

"There, by that table. He could be injured."

Speedy was a risk-taker, but maybe he was right. Greco knew full well that there was no body. It was a ploy to justify breaking in. Greco wasn't happy about it but he needed the case to break, and Mickey Dent was all they had.

"Okay, get us inside."

Another filthy hovel littered with beer cans and cigarette ends. The flat was empty. Speedy searched the rooms.

"Nice laptop here, sir. Do we take it?"

Greco didn't reply. They'd need a damn good reason to remove anything and they didn't have a warrant. Strictly speaking they were in this flat illegally. He walked across to a chest of drawers. The top drawer contained bundles of old papers, the next a number of old CDs. But there was also something wrapped in a cloth. Greco took a pair of latex gloves from his pocket and carefully lifted it out. It was a gun, complete with silencer. Searching further he found the box of bullets that went with it. He held it out for Speedy to see.

"Look what we've got here."

Greco had a closer look at the other drawers. At the back of the bottom one, he found a notebook. He held it up. "Adam Crompton's! It has his name on the front."

"That makes Dent our knifeman. What's the gun, a Glock?"

"Yes," Greco said, and put it back. Grace's instinct was spot on. He should learn to trust her more. "We can't take anything. First we need a warrant, and we need to get the Duggan out here too. This place must be gone over with a fine toothcomb."

Before they left, Greco rang the station. He wanted the flat taped off and watched. "I'll make my way back. You wait for the uniforms. I don't want anything in here touched until we've got that warrant."

On the windowsill, Greco saw a photo of Mickey Dent with his sister, Michelle. He took a quick snap with the camera on his mobile. One for the incident board.

Chapter 22

Grace was speaking to the team. "I don't think it was just a matter of not understanding English. He was being deliberately evasive. The lad we saw was very young. He was unkempt, thin. At a pinch, he could have been on placement from school, but I seriously doubt it."

"Joel, ring round the local schools, see what you can find out." Greco tapped the board. "The warrant to search Mickey Dent's flat came through. We'll know shortly if the gun Speedy and I found is the one we're looking for. In the meantime, we need to find him." He handed Grace the photo he'd printed out.

"I think this is your weirdo."

"The clothes are different, but stick this ruffian in a suit, fix his hair, and bingo! What did I tell you? I knew he was a wrong 'un."

"Speedy, ring his sister, see if she can help. He might have contacted her. See if she knows what he's been up to recently." Greco was trying to piece this together. Crompton had been killed by the Knifeman, Tanner and Shaw had been shot. Did finding the notebook mean that Dent was responsible for the lot?

"Who do we reckon Dent was working for?"

"I'd say Shaw," Grace replied. "I think he did the knifings for him, and then they fell out. Dent wanted to get even for something."

"It must have been something big," Speedy added. "He killed the pair of them, Tanner and Shaw."

Greco was thinking hard. "If Dent killed Jamal Ali and the other lad that means Shaw was involved in bringing the illegals in."

"Jamal Ali and the other lad escaped. Shaw wanted them dealt with and hired Dent," Grace added. "Perhaps Shaw didn't pay him enough."

"Leah, your informant said that the Knifeman was new, an unknown."

She nodded. "He told me that Slicer had deliberately gone for someone unknown so that he wouldn't be linked to him, and could be got rid of once it was over."

"Perhaps Dent got wind of that and decided to do Slicer and Tanner before they could get to him," Speedy suggested.

That made sense. Greco gave it a few moments' thought. "The different weapons could indicate that he was trying to shift the blame elsewhere."

"And it worked," Leah added. "Rumours of a rift between Costello and Shaw were doing the rounds. Tanner and Shaw's murders were seen as Costello's retribution. But my informant reckons Costello is in no state to rock the boat. He's ill, and paying for a lot of private treatment."

"Hence Horton and Sadie," noted Greco. "But we must not forget Todoran's part in all this. He was in the club last night talking to Shaw. What did he want? Where is he now? The man is dangerous. He's someone else we need to find urgently."

Grace looked at him. "We still don't really know what this is all about." Greco caught her eye. She was right.

"We might be able to explain away Dent, and why he did what he did, but why were the lads being brought here in the first place?"

"Modern slavery. That factory we went to is a prime example," Joel suggested. "I bet there are dozens of them around Manchester, all over the country in fact. It's a very lucrative trade."

Grace nodded. "So where does the Rashid Clinic fit in?"

That had been puzzling Greco too. "Horton is reputed to have a gambling problem. Shaw may have persuaded him to treat the lads when they became ill."

Grace nodded. "It's a theory. Tony Rouse found out and threatened to expose the clinic. Then got Slicer on his back for his trouble."

"Sir!" A uniformed officer from downstairs was at the door. "A group of workmen have found a body at the back of the Lansdowne. The old mill on Cotton Street."

The team looked at one another. Rouse or Dent?

Greco nodded at Speedy. "We'll go and take a look."

* * *

The old red-brick mill sat desolate and crumbling in the rain. What was left of the windows were rattling in the wind. The door was hanging off its hinges. A huge sign on the rusting gates proclaimed the building to be unsafe. Various pieces of heavy digging equipment were in evidence. It looked like the place was about to be razed to the ground.

The team from the Duggan was already there. The body had been found an hour ago and they'd got straight on it.

"He's young, shot through the head. Nasty." Bob Bowers shuddered. "Get these on and I'll show you." He handed the detectives white paper coveralls and gloves.

They entered the dirty, abandoned mill. The scene was gruesome. The young man was lying on his back, tied to a wooden pallet. The concrete floor below his head was covered in blood.

Bob Bowers lifted one of the victim's hands. "Torture. One hand completely crushed, plus a finger on the other one."

"Not done after death in an attempt to destroy prints?" asked Greco.

"No, the injuries to both hands were sustained prior to death — blood and bruising, see? I'd say your killer wanted answers. But this is most certainly what killed him." He pointed to the vicious-looking wound in Mickey Dent's temple. "I'll do the PM later today. You can attend if you want but I'll have the results on the system as quick as I can."

The crime scene investigators were everywhere, scouring every inch of the floor and examining what equipment had been left in the place.

One of them called out from near the doorway. "There is a small amount of blood on the floor over here!"

"Too far from where he was shot. Could be the killer's," Speedy said hopefully. "God knows we could do with a break."

"Or it could be that the lad was making a run for it and the killer stopped him," said the investigator.

Greco hoped that it was Speedy who was right. "I realise it's not the best of jobs, but would you tell his sister? You know her. She will need a friendly face. Don't tell her the details, but ask if she can help. Tell us where he went, who his friends were, you know the stuff."

Speedy nodded. "Who did this, sir? Slicer's dead, the local villains are still in turmoil. So who are we looking at?"

"Costello — possibly?" But Greco was doubtful about this. "We must also consider Todoran's part in it. He was also in the club last night. Shaw might have decided Dent's usefulness was at an end, and decided to set Todoran on him."

Greco shouted to one of the forensic team, "Any sign of a mobile?" The man shook his head.

"What are the chances of finding him?" asked Speedy. "We still haven't located Tony Rouse. Although things have moved on since he disappeared."

"We still need to find him. He knows what this is about. You go and see Michelle. I'll go back to the station and get Grace, and then we'll go and have a talk with Jean Smethurst about Rouse."

Greco left Speedy to it. He'd more than likely get one of the uniforms to give him a lift. But a walk would do his sergeant no harm, and Michelle's workplace wasn't far away.

The brutality of Dent's killing shocked Greco. Whoever had done that was an animal. But despite his reputation, he didn't think it was Costello. Greco had read about that villain's methods. Costello didn't leave his victims lying around for the police to find. He would have got the information he wanted and then the body would have been disposed of, never to see the light of day again. Mickey Dent would have become just another missing person. There was no evidence that whoever had done this had been in any hurry. So either the killer wasn't bothered, or he wasn't particularly forensically aware. That left a big question mark. Apart from Costello or one of his mob, there was no one else in the frame.

And what information had the killer wanted from Dent? What did the lad know that was so valuable?

* * *

"Take the next right at the lights." Grace was reading the address Joel had given her. "She lives in Blackley, the better part too. Near the park."

"The gun and notebook found at Dent's flat have gone to the Duggan. Message Roxy and tell her we need to know as soon as possible if it's the one that killed Tanner and Shaw," Greco said.

Grace grinned. "You were taking a risk, breaking into that flat. Not your usual style. Good to know that even you can break the rules sometimes."

"Speedy's idea. He might fly by the seat of his pants, but there are times when his style of policing is useful."

"You don't look very happy."

"You wouldn't either if you'd seen that body. The poor lad suffered. One of his hands was completely smashed. The brute must have used something hard and made of metal."

"A fight between killers. Remember, Dent knifed those young lads."

"I still don't like it. Even he didn't deserve that."

Grace changed the subject. "Are we going to talk about what happened in Brighton? We've only been back a day or so now, and it's as if you've wiped the entire episode from your memory."

He hadn't, but he was trying very hard to do just that. The problem was, he liked Grace. If his personal circumstances were different he would be up for a relationship. But he still had Suzy constantly in his head. It wasn't something he could fix quickly. "What is there to talk about?"

"Us for a start. We slept together. You might say you're not interested but that's not true, is it?"

"This is neither the time nor the place. And I don't think you should think in terms of there being an '*us.*'"

"It never is the right time with you."

That could be true. In truth, he was terrified of having a relationship with anyone. He could not go through that experience again, losing someone, like he'd lost Suzy.

"Leave it be, Grace."

"I was going to invite you and Matilda round for dinner one night. The girls would love it, and we could talk."

"I'm not ready. You're a lovely young woman, but I'm just not ready."

"That's not true, Stephen. No one had your arm up your back. You slept with me because you wanted to."

"Can we drop this, please?"

He heard her impatient sigh. But what could he do? He'd made a huge mistake in Brighton. Why couldn't Grace simply accept that?

"We're here, number forty. You can park down there." She pointed to a spot a few yards away.

They walked to the front door in silence. Greco knew that Grace was annoyed with him. He didn't know how to handle this. He'd never been any good where relationships with women were concerned. She thought him cold, berated him for his lack of feeling, but that wasn't what he was like at all. The simple truth was that he was scared stiff of loving anyone again. Police work was a dangerous business.

"It won't go away, Stephen," Grace said, as they reached the front door. "I won't let it."

***

Jean Smethurst looked them up and down. "I've been expecting you. You are police, I take it?"

Grace and Greco showed her their badges, and Greco got straight to the point. "Have you seen Tony Rouse in the past week?"

"You'd better come in." She led the way into the sitting room.

The house was neat and tidy, spotless in fact, and Greco had no qualms about sitting down. This was very different from the others they'd been to during the course of this case.

"I told Tony that I wouldn't lie. I don't see the point. You will get to the truth sooner or later and anyway, he has done nothing wrong."

"Has he spoken to you about his antics over the past few days? We've been to his apartment in Spinningfields—"

165

"Then you will have seen what he did," she interrupted. "The gunshot in the bathroom. The blood came from a joint of pork I defrosted. Stupid fool! I told him so at the time. The gun, incidentally, is registered to him. He needed time to disappear. He reckoned it would buy him that. The people after him wanted blood."

"Do you know who these people are?" Greco asked her.

"No. Tony didn't talk to me about his work, even though I'd worked with him at the paper. So I do understand the pitfalls."

"He came here to lie low?" Grace asked.

"Yes. Very few people know about us. We used to go out with Adam and his wife, Molly. They knew, but no one from the paper."

"Where is he now?" asked Greco.

"I don't know. If I did, believe me, I'd tell you. I want Tony safe as much as you do."

Everything about her — the body language, the way she spoke — told them that Jean Smethurst was telling the truth. Both detectives knew it, but they still had to push.

And so Greco pushed. "Are you sure? Because if you do, and you don't tell us, that is obstruction. It carries its own penalties."

"I know that, I'm not stupid! Tony was here up until last night, and then he left. He'd had his mobile turned off for days. He was paranoid that if he left it on, you'd track him. Last night he turned it on and there was a message. He didn't say who it was from," she added before they had a chance to ask her. "He simply gathered his things and left. I've heard nothing since."

"Is his mobile on now?"

"No. I have tried ringing him."

"Do you have any idea where he might be, or who that message was from?" asked Greco.

"No, but I'm sure you can find out."

She was right. The moment they were back in the car, Greco would get onto the station and ask Joel Hough to do just that.

"He has his apartment, and sometimes he stays in that hovel his mother rents. But I doubt he'd go there. Too many people after his blood on that estate."

"Has he said anything about what he is investigating?" asked Grace. "We know some of it, but there's a big part we know nothing about. People have been killed, Adam Crompton for one."

"I saw that on the local news. I wanted to ring his wife but Tony said not to. He wouldn't tell me anything. Said it was safer not to know. But whatever it was, it turned his stomach."

"Has he ever mentioned the Rashid Clinic to you?" Grace asked her.

"That place! Yes, he's talked about it. Tony didn't say a lot, just that the place should be closed down."

"And he didn't say why?"

She shook her head.

"He might come back," Greco continued. "If he does you must contact us. I'm not exaggerating when I say that his life may depend on it." He handed her his card.

Chapter 23

Day 7

Unable to sleep, Greco had spent most of the night going over the case notes. He'd arrived at the station early, had a long telephone conversation with Roxy Atkins at the Duggan and then prepared a short report for each member of the team.

"A knife was found on the body of Mickey Dent," he began, handing out the sheets. "It's being checked for DNA, and against the wounds on the dead boys."

"Looks highly likely that we've found our knifeman. He killed the lads and shot Tanner and Shaw."

Greco shook his head. "It might not be that simple, Speedy. We found the gun that killed them in Dent's flat, but we mustn't jump to conclusions. He might have been keeping it for someone else."

"My informant said that the Glock had been sold to someone young." Leah reminded them. "Dent fits that bill."

Greco looked at Leah. "He might have done the buying, but the gun may not have been for him. You were told about a rift between Shaw and Costello. That could mean that Dent was working for Costello. Dent was a very small cog, even in Shaw's tiny piece of Costello's patch. Would the big man trust the job of taking out his enemies to someone like him, an unknown, untried youngster?" He was thinking out loud.

Leah nodded. "Not his style, granted."

"CSI found a metal bar in the mill," Greco continued. "Doctor Atkins is still testing but she thinks it was one of the weapons used on Dent. There are fibres on the bar. She will see if they match those on Dent's clothing. He has a nasty bruise between his shoulder blades. From where the bar was found it looks as if it was thrown at him, perhaps to stop him running away. A heavy lump hammer was also found. This has traces of tissue and blood on it. They're testing it for Dent's DNA. This was the weapon used on his hands." Greco cleared his throat. "The bullet that killed him was not from the Glock."

"Do we know if the gun has been used previously?" Leah asked.

"The Duggan are checking."

"So what now?" asked Grace. "Slicer, Tanner and now Dent are all dead. Who are we left with?"

"Cezar Todoran," replied Greco. "We know he's involved somewhere. We think he brings the lads in from the Syrian-Turkish border, drives them across Europe and dumps them in Calais."

"How do they get to England?" asked Leah.

"Amani Ali told us they are stowed away in lorries. Todoran is involved in that too."

"Surely transport coming in from Calais is checked these days?" Joel Hough said.

"That's the theory," Grace replied. "But the fact is, these people are getting through."

"I did alert Border Control," Greco told them. "I had a conversation while Grace and I were still in Brighton. I will contact them again. Hopefully they've upped security."

"The smugglers are very clever. The lorries are often adapted to fit in two dozen or more at a time. I saw a documentary on the telly. Lorries built with a space between the outside and fake internal walls. Just enough space for people to sit." Speedy shook his head.

"There is an alert out for Todoran," Greco told them. "If he shows his face, we've got him."

"Perhaps, but will he talk to us? I've had a run-in with that man. He's big, ugly and I'd say capable of anything." Grace shuddered.

"His DNA is on record. If that patch of blood by the mill door is his, he'll go down for a long time," Greco told Grace. "And that's without adding in the trafficking."

Leah was looking thoughtful. "Back to the problem of who killed Shaw and his driver, sir. Dent was new. But what if he was hungry for power? What if he killed Tanner so that he could get closer to Shaw? When Shaw wouldn't give him what he wanted, he did him too."

"Didn't work though, did it? But we'll keep an open mind for now. Knowing more about the Glock will help matters."

Joel looked up from his screen. "Sir, we've just had an email back from the IT bloke at the Duggan. Adam Crompton's browser history has thrown up something. He was searching for hotels in Cheshire. He checked out the website of a guest house in Hazel Grove. It looks like he booked a room."

"Get the address." Greco looked at Grace. "We'll go and take a look. Leah, Speedy, you find out all you can about Hussain Textiles. Joel, get onto the schools. Let's rule out the placement idea. Anything else from the Duggan, let me know at once."

"That last message, sir," Joel began. "It was from an unregistered pay-as-you-go mobile. The message was simple — *'you are dead.'*"

No help at all. Rouse ran because the message scared him. Greco could only hope they found him before the sender did.

* * *

"You look ropey again."

As blunt as ever. Greco shook his head and handed her the keys. "I've had precious little sleep. My head won't stop."

"Mine neither, but I bet the reasons are very different."

"Don't bring that up again, Grace." He was sick and tired of her going on about what had happened between them. All he wanted to do was forget, pretend it had never happened. Even Pat kept asking what was wrong. He hadn't mentioned Grace, but Pat had brought her up. She wanted chapter and verse about how they'd spent their time in Brighton. Apparently when he spoke about Grace, he smiled and appeared more relaxed, so Pat had jumped to the conclusion that he liked her. Which he did. But it was not that simple. He needed time to mull things over.

"At least give it a rest until we've sorted this case. How far is Hazel Grove?"

"It's on the A6, beyond Stockport. If the traffic is kind, it should take us about twenty minutes. That place where Rouse is staying, it's a backstreet guest house. Cheap and cheerful."

"He's hiding. He's hardly going to make a show of himself, is he?"

"The big question is, who's he hiding from? Shaw and his mob, or Todoran? Wonder if he knows Shaw is dead? What do you think?"

"I don't know what to think. I just hope that Rouse is honest with us for once."

The traffic along the A6 through the town of Hazel Grove was slow. The street they were looking for was off

171

to the left, near the railway station. After a frustrating stop-start drive they spotted the street they wanted.

Greco nodded to a large detached house a good fifty yards or so away. "That's the place. We'll park here. I'll take the front door, you go around the back. He might decide to run for it."

The front doors were open and led into a wide hallway. There was a desk with a bell, but there was no one about. A door behind the desk had a 'private' sign hanging from it. The owner's rooms no doubt. Greco tapped on it. A man opened it and smiled at them both.

"Are you looking for a room?"

Greco showed him his badge. "No, I'm looking for this man." He showed him a photo of Rouse.

"Mr Campbell. He is staying here."

"How long?"

"A couple of days, but I don't know much about him. Not left the room and had all his meals up there. He is in room twenty, top of the stairs. Do you want me to give him a knock for you? Ask him to come down?"

"No, I'll surprise him. Has he had any other visitors?" The man shook his head. At that moment Grace appeared at the other end of the hallway.

"This is my colleague. We'll go up together." The man didn't ask questions, but simply nodded in the direction they should go.

"Is he in?" asked Grace.

"Yes. He arrived a couple of days ago and he's never left the room."

Rouse was obviously scared. Greco and Grace made their way up the stairs quietly. They stood outside the door and listened for a few moments. They could hear music. Rouse must have the radio on.

"Do we knock?" Grace whispered.

Greco nodded and tapped lightly. "Mr Campbell!" With any luck, Rouse would think it was the owner and answer.

It worked. Seconds later, Rouse stood in the doorway. He froze when he saw the two detectives. Before he could react, Greco had his foot in the door, and a second later they were inside.

Greco stood with his back to the door, blocking any attempt at escape. "The elusive Mr Rouse. We've been looking for you for days. You're a tricky chap to pin down. What, or who, are you hiding from?"

Rouse went to the window and looked up and down the street. "If you can find me, so can they. You shouldn't have come here, you'll get us all killed."

"Who are you talking about?" asked Greco.

"The mob that are after me. The bastards trading in human flesh." He turned and faced them. "You've investigated, you know what I'm talking about. I saw things, asked questions, so now I'm a marked man. They know I've spoken to you lot. Adam was killed as a warning to me. I was supposed to stop, give up the story, lighten up. But I didn't. The day I left Manchester, I had literally minutes to get away."

"You shot a hole in your own bathroom wall and smeared it with pig's blood!" Grace told him. "How was that supposed to help?"

"With luck, they'd have thought I was dead. Presumed that Slicer had had me taken out like the lads and Adam. It worked, up to a point. But you lot kept sniffing around. I know they are still looking. The newspaper office was visited. They scared Anna witless."

"No one reported it," said Grace.

"She was too frightened. They told her if she went to the police they'd kill her."

"You went to Brighton, spoke to Amani Ali. You hurt her." Greco crossed his arms.

"That was a mistake. I meant her no harm. I simply wanted to talk. It was her kid brother that got knifed. I hoped to get some background, that was all. I grabbed her arm to stop her running. She struggled and screamed. Said I'd broken it."

"She wouldn't speak to you?"

"She was too scared. Bright girl!"

"Who is it you're afraid of, Mr Rouse? Shaw and his driver are dead, so they are no threat to you. We have it on good authority that Costello is ill. So, I ask again, just who is so terrifying?"

He looked them up and down. Was he trying to decide whether to confide in them? Finally he shook his head. "No, I value my life. If I tell you what I know, they'll kill me. This operation that I have been investigating is big. The people at the top would think nothing of taking us all out to save their skins — me and the pair of you — if it suited them. I'm about to do a deal with one of the dailies. The money they are paying will set me up in a new life abroad."

Greco heaved a sigh and sat down on a chair. "It'd take a whole lot of money to do that, Mr Rouse. It would be far better to speak to us. Tell us what you know and we will protect you. We'll put you somewhere safe until we've got whoever you're so scared of under lock and key."

Rouse shook his head. "That won't happen. They're far too clever. They've got their lethal tentacles everywhere, even the nick. Besides which they'll have alibis coming out of their ears before you lot get your backsides in gear."

They were getting nowhere. "Mr Rouse, you are giving me no choice but to arrest you. Lock you up until you talk to us."

"On what grounds? I've done nowt wrong, you've got nothing on me."

Greco snapped back, "At the very least you have obstructed our investigation, withheld important information. You know things, you've admitted as much. Now talk to me, or I'll take you back to the station."

Grace's mobile rang. It was Joel Hough. She went out onto the landing to take the call. Moments later, she was back in Rouse's room.

"We need to get going, sir. Something's happened. A kid from that factory has been found. He'd been taken to Manchester General. We are keeping an eye on him and he wants to talk to someone."

Rouse made no comment.

Greco handcuffed him, and they led him, protesting, out to the car. Greco wanted to keep the man safe. Put him somewhere where he could talk to him without having to scour Greater Manchester to do so.

Once they were on their way, Rouse leaned forward.

"This kid. Where's he from?"

"Sorry, Rouse, I can't tell you that," Greco looked at the man's grim face. "Irritating, isn't it?"

"Doesn't matter. I can guess. He'll be an illegal. He's either scarpered from some backstreet sweatshop, or that hospital in Chorlton. Which is it?"

Greco smiled. "No comment."

Chapter 24

"The lad climbed out through a broken window," Joel explained to Greco. "He gashed his arm badly. The nurse who rang said he was going for an X-ray to make sure there was no glass in there, but it would definitely need stitching."

"What was her name?"

"Molly Crompton, sir."

"Rouse will be okay in the cells for a while. Get him some tea and a sandwich. The minute he decides he wants to talk, call me."

Grace looked impatient. "I wonder if it was the lad we saw when we visited. He must have guessed we were police when he saw how agitated his boss was. We need to get back to that factory before they clean the place up."

"We'll speak to the lad first. See what he can tell us. We can't just go barging in there without solid evidence," Greco told her.

"Interesting that it was Crompton's wife who rang us."

"She's as keen to get to the bottom of this as we are."

They drove to the hospital in silence, each mulling over the day's events. Grace was worried about the lad and what he might have been through. Greco was irritated at Rouse's refusal to help them.

They parked up and went to the renal unit to find Molly Crompton. She was standing at the nurse's station on the corridor.

"He's not very well at all. A badly cut arm and a nasty infection." So much for patient confidentiality. "He's young, about sixteen I'd say. He says he's alone and I've no reason to disbelieve him. So there is no adult we can call on. I have contacted social services and immigration . . ." She shrugged. "I had no choice. I suspect he's in the country illegally. Apart from which, I'm concerned about what has happened to him. Whoever was keeping that boy needs punishing. Animals shouldn't be kept in such conditions."

"Does he speak English?"

"Fortunately he does."

"Can we see him?" asked Greco.

She nodded and led the way. "His name is Farid. He thinks he's been in the country about three months. He got here in a heavy goods vehicle. He thought he was going to start a new life. He wouldn't say where he was from."

The boy was lying on a bed in the renal ward hooked up to a drip. His dark eyes went wide when he spotted the detectives.

"Don't send me back," he pleaded.

Grace spoke to him gently. "We are not going to do that, Farid. You will be looked after here, and made well again."

"Will you tell us how you got here, Farid?" asked Greco. "We think you were brought here by some bad people who have done wicked things."

The boy fell silent for a few moments. His eyes searched Greco's face. Then he seemed to come to a decision.

"I was taken from our village with some others when the soldiers came. Me and some other boys escaped. We made it to the Turkish border. There we met a man. He was well known among the refugees. If he liked you, he would help."

"Did he ask for money?" Grace asked.

"A little, whatever you could afford. He said he would take us to Calais. For most of the boys that was it, Calais and no further. But for others, me included, it was different. I don't know why that was, but I agreed to come to England to work. The man said he would find me a job, but only if I was healthy."

Greco looked at Grace. This again. "You had blood tests?" he asked.

The boy nodded. "The man said that if the tests were okay, he would bring me to England."

"Did you start work at that factory straight away?"

Farid looked at Grace and shook his head.

"I was kept somewhere, I don't know where. There were others like me. No one knew what was going to happen. One boy said we were in the south of England. He kept trying to get away. He had family in London. While we were there we had more blood tests."

That meant a hospital. "These other boys, do you remember any of their names?" asked Greco.

"I only remember Jamal. He was from my village too. We were together most of the time but when we reached England, we got separated. He was found work near his sister. He was okay, happy to be with her. He tried to get away from the men, to disappear. He kicked off many times. Eventually they locked him up. Wouldn't let him talk to anyone. Soon after that he was gone. The man said Jamal had been punished, that we'd never see him again. I never knew what really happened."

Greco decided that this wasn't the time to tell him. "Jamal had the same tests as you?"

Farid nodded. "The man who'd brought us to England said we were very lucky to have been chosen."

"What happened next? How did you end up at the factory?"

He looked at Greco, his eyes wide again. He moved his head from side to side. "I hate that place. They use us like slaves. We are not allowed to leave. We have to sleep in a room at the back with nothing but sleeping bags."

Molly Crompton came in. "Farid has talked for long enough. He really does need to rest. He is quite poorly."

Grace nodded. "He'll be worn out, undernourished and very rundown."

"That we can cope with. It's the infection that's proving challenging. We are doing tests but it looks like he's got MRSA in his wound."

Greco was puzzled. "What wound? Not the one in his arm, that's too recent."

"Sometime during the last month Farid has undergone surgery."

"What type of surgery?"

Molly Crompton looked at Greco. Her expression was hard. "He was reluctant to tell us at first. Apparently he'd been threatened, told to keep his mouth shut, but we did a CT scan. The lad has had a kidney removed."

* * *

Once they were back at the station, Greco arranged for Farid to be kept under guard at the hospital. He didn't want anyone abducting the lad, neither did he want him taking off on his own.

Grace and Greco walked along the corridor to the incident room.

"What does it mean?" she said. "Why would anyone take a kidney?"

Greco's voice was hard with anger. "To give to someone else. I want another word with Rouse. You go and tell the team what we've just learned."

"That would take a surgeon who knew what he was doing. Plus an operating theatre, facilities. A medical team." Grace took hold of Greco's arm and stopped walking. "The Rashid Clinic! This is down to them, isn't it?"

Greco didn't reply. Instead he turned on his heel and walked off towards the cells. He had Tony Rouse taken to an interview room.

They sat staring at each other. "Organ donation — or rather organ theft. Is that what this is all about?"

"Clever copper, aren't you? It took you long enough though."

"How long have you known?"

Rouse's eyes narrowed. "Who've you got in custody?"

Greco looked at him. "Why? Who should we have brought in?"

"Look, I'm saying nowt until the people behind this are under lock and key. You might think I'm safe in here, but if I talk and they find out, I'm a dead man, locked up or not."

The only man Greco was aware of who had the power to reach even into the police force, was Costello.

"Is Vinny Costello behind this?"

Rouse laughed. "He's finished, too sick to leave his house."

"So who?"

"Just who have you brought in, copper? You know what's going on now. So how did you find out?"

Greco would have to tell him something or he'd get nowhere.

"We have a teenage boy in hospital. He has a kidney missing. And I don't think he gave it up willingly."

"He's spoken to you? Told you who did that to him?"

Greco shook his head. "I doubt he knows."

"You could be right. But he'll know that Romanian bastard. Ask the lad about him."

"Todoran? Is it him behind this?"

"So you know him too." Rouse gave Greco a bitter smile. "Not one to cross. A hard man with no conscience. But he hasn't got the brains. He finds them, brings them in. Got it down to a fine art."

"Who is Todoran working for?"

"Whoever pays him the most. Currently that is the new big boss. Not that they will have ever met. I'll lay odds that Todoran got all his instructions from someone further down the chain." Rouse fell silent. He stared at Greco and shook his head.

"No more. I've said enough. I value my life too much."

"This new big boss, he's taken over from Costello?" Rouse said nothing.

"What harm can it do to tell me? The name will be on the street before long anyway."

"Not yet it won't. Doesn't suit. Costello is ill. It is rumoured he won't see out the month. Then it will be on the street, not before."

"The new boss — he is behind this?"

"Get lost, copper. I'm saying nothing else."

"Bad decision, Rouse. Speak to us and we can protect you. Refuse and you're on your own again."

"I'll take my chances."

Greco went back to the incident room. On his way, he bumped into McCabe.

"That reporter, Rouse. We can't hold him."

Greco was well aware of that. But with McCabe on the case he'd have no choice but to release him sooner rather than later. "I hoped he'd speak to us. Rouse knows things, the names of people we should know about."

"You don't know that for sure, Stephen. You think he does, and you might be right. But you can't keep him here any longer. Have you spoken to him? Given him the chance to tell you what he knows?"

"Yes, and he won't budge."

"Then get rid. Throw him back to the wolves, but have him watched."

Greco nodded. He knew that McCabe was right.

The incident room was noisy. Grace had brought the others up to date with events, and the theories were bouncing around.

Greco spoke to Joel Hough. "Get on to downstairs. Tell them to release Rouse. I want you to follow him. Take a uniform and don't let him out of your sight."

"What if he sees us?"

"He's a frightened man. I don't think he'll argue much if he sees police on his tail."

Speedy chipped in. "It's got to be that clinic, sir. Horton was a renal specialist in his previous life."

"We can't go storming in. We still don't have the proof we need. The boy, Farid, will talk to us. Unfortunately he needs time to recover a little, and he may not know names."

"He might recognise faces though," Leah suggested. "We could show him photos of Todoran, Horton and Rashid and see what he says."

Greco nodded. "We'll do that. But what Rouse said makes me think that it is not so simple."

"I thought Rouse didn't speak to you," said Grace.

"He didn't. He's too scared. But he did say that even locked up in here he reckons he's still not safe. He said that whoever is behind this can still get to him. Some new big boss who is running Costello's empire. Horton and his chums can't do that. And Todoran strikes me as a loner, a man who sells his services to the highest bidder."

"Someone new?" Leah was puzzled.

"According to Rouse, Costello is gravely ill, and out of the picture."

"So who is orchestrating this?" asked Grace. "And while we're at it, we might ask ourselves how big an operation is this? Was Farid the first, for example? If not, how many other poor buggers have fallen victim to illegal surgery?"

Greco had been thinking the same, and he had a bad feeling about it. Jamal Ali had had tests, and possibly the other lad that had been killed. There could have been dozens before them.

Speedy looked around at them. "That man, Hamid Khan, the one with the kidney problems. He was having treatment at the clinic. What we didn't understand was why. He could get all the dialysis he needed at the local NHS hospital. There aren't any drugs or procedures that would sort him. He'd reached the stage where his only chance was a transplant."

Greco stared at him for a few moments.

"So they promised him one."

The team were silent as the implications of this hit home. "For all we know, that clinic could be doing it on a grand scale. Bringing the lads in, testing them, hiving off the likely suspects and feeding the rest to the backstreet sweatshops."

Speedy frowned. "It's a nightmare scenario, sir. Wonder what they charge?"

"For a kidney? Who knows? Hamid Khan's wife did say they'd paid a lot of money."

Suddenly Speedy did one of his loud whistles. "There could be an entire black market out there! With the Rashid Clinic at the centre of it. Bring the lads in and take their organs. The poor buggers are being used for spare parts."

"We need to know more about tissue matching. These lads are all from a particular ethnic background. We need to know if that restricts which ethnic groups the organs can be used for." Greco looked at Gareth Dobbs. "Do some urgent research and let me know what you find."

Chapter 25

Day 8

The team were silent as Greco briefed them early the following morning. "We gather evidence and then we strike. We need a solid case, or anyone we bring in will walk. Grace and I will speak to the lad, Farid, again. This time I will show him the photos of that lot." He nodded at the board. "If he recognises any of them, particularly Horton or Rashid, then we are good to go. I will get a warrant and we'll go through that clinic with a fine toothcomb."

The team were listening intently. They all knew that this had to be done right. "We do have a warrant to search the factory, Hussain's Textiles. Leah, you and Speedy go and clear the place. An officer from immigration will go with you, plus uniformed officers. I want that man Hussain arrested and put in the cells. He must know something about all this. Not only does he get the rejected boys as part of his workforce, but he gets them back after the operation too."

"What about Todoran?" asked Speedy.

"We are still looking for him. Anything from the Duggan?" Greco looked around.

Speedy checked the nearest computer and shook his head.

"The blood found in the mill, we need to know if it is Todoran's. We also need confirmation about the knife found on Mickey Dent." Greco looked at Speedy. "Did you speak to his sister, Michelle? Did she have anything helpful to say?"

"No, sir, nothing she'd admit to." He looked sheepish. "She's been staying with me. She won't say, but I think Michelle was feeding her brother information. She had access to my notebook. She could have told him anything."

"Where's she staying now?"

"She's gone back to her own place, sir. I tackled her about it. I'm afraid it hasn't done much for the relationship." He shrugged.

"I did that research you asked for, sir," Gareth Dobbs told Greco. "It seems that people from ethnic minorities wait longer on average for a transplant. Organs are in short supply."

"A ready market — providing the patients can come up with the money."

Leah's mobile rang. Greco waited while she dealt with the call. It was Joel Hough. "Rouse spent the night at his apartment in Spinningfields. But he's on the move again this morning. He has gone to the Grapes pub, sir. He knows my informant. If he's looking for him, then Rouse is after information."

"Is he likely to get it?"

Leah finished the call. "It depends on how much money Rouse is prepared to pay. My man's info is reliable, but there is no loyalty. He'll sell what he knows to the highest bidder."

"Ring Joel back. Tell him he must not lose Rouse."

* * *

Farid was a little better. He was sitting up in bed when Greco and Grace arrived on the ward.

"He's eaten and been quite talkative," Molly Crompton told them. "He also rang a member of his family who is currently in Turkey. He seems happier."

"The infection?"

"We are treating that with some serious drugs. We'll see."

Greco greeted the boy with a smile. "We are the detectives who were here yesterday. We had a little chat."

The boy nodded.

"We want to find the people who did this to you," Greco told him. "Have you remembered anything? Any little detail will help."

Farid shook his head. "Each time I was moved it was at night and they covered my head."

"You might not know any names or remember the places, but you might recognise some of these faces."

Grace handed Farid the photos one by one. First Mickey Dent. The lad shook his head. Next Slicer Shaw. Nothing there either. The third photo was that of Faisal Rashid. Farid stared at it for several seconds before looking up at Greco. "I think I might have seen him."

"What about this man?" Greco handed him the image of Jason Horton. Farid gave a little scream, and let the photo fall to the floor.

"He is the devil! It was him who did this," he said, putting his hand to his side.

"Are you sure it was him? Did anyone you were with use his name?"

"No, but I remember his face. He was very handsome but full of wickedness. He spoke to me as if I was nothing. He gave me drugs, operated on me against my will."

"Was this in a hospital?"

"Yes, but I was taken there at night so I didn't see much. When I got there, he spoke to me and then I was drugged."

That was all Greco needed. "He will be caught and punished for what he has done. You are quite safe now."

Molly Crompton stopped them on their way out. "Helpful?"

Greco smiled back. "We are getting somewhere at last." As they walked back to the car, he made the phone call to arrange the warrant.

* * *

Speedy, Leah and an immigration officer called Margaret Brown pulled up behind a van full of uniformed officers in front of the main entrance to Hussain's Textiles. The uniforms split up, some going off to the rear of the building. Two more vans pulled up beside them to take the illegal workers away to be processed.

Speedy banged on the main doors, while Leah waited impatiently beside him.

"No one is going to answer," she decided. She nodded to a uniform who launched a battering ram at the door. Seconds later they were in.

The reception area was as messy as Grace had described it, littered with boxes and rubbish. Speedy led the way down the corridor to the rooms at the back. They could hear raised voices, and a man shouting. The uniformed officers who'd tackled the rear of the building were already inside. Suddenly Speedy heard a gunshot.

"We need bulletproof vests," Leah hissed to the uniform behind her. He scuttled off back to the van.

Speedy dropped to his knees. "Get down!" They heard another shot and a man screamed.

"I hope that's not one of ours." Speedy craned his neck to see what was going on. "It's one bloke," he whispered to Leah. "He has his back to us, about halfway down the corridor and he's blocking the door into the workroom. I could rush him, send him flying."

Leah grabbed his arm. "Not worth the risk, Speedy. If he turns and fires, you're dead."

"Uniform are in there," he hissed back. "For all we know, one of our own could be injured, or worse."

"We do this by the book. We get an armed response unit. We get the vests on, and then we'll see."

But Speedy wasn't prepared to wait. He gave Leah a backward glance then made a dash for it. He charged towards the man who was holding the gun. His luck held. Speedy dived forward and made a wild grab for the man's legs, and he fell forward heavily. Speedy heard the gun rattle across the concrete floor. Uniform were on him straight away.

Leah ran forward and stood beside Speedy. "Bloody fool! You took a huge risk there."

"Worked though, didn't it?" He grinned.

"Anyone injured?"

Speedy nodded at one of the uniforms. "He hit Alan over there with the butt of his gun. Apart from him, no. He fired into the ceiling." Speedy pointed to a large hole, spilling plaster. He looked around. The room they were in, and the two adjoining ones, were full of sewing machines. At least two dozen young men were cowering beneath the tables.

"Round them up," Leah told the nearest uniform. "Margaret Brown, the immigration officer, is in the van outside. She'll tell you where to take them."

Speedy held up a hand. "Not all of them. We want him and the bloke hiding in the office over there. This bloke is the one we saw the other day, and I reckon that's Hussain himself."

Leah found Greco's mobile number and told him what had happened. "We've secured the factory and got the workers in custody. They'll be processed by immigration. This place is being searched now. I'll get the people from the Duggan down. See what they turn up."

Greco sounded pleased. "We've had a positive outcome from Farid too. Grace and I are on our way to the Rashid Clinic."

* * *

"I need money." Cezar Todoran stared at Jason Horton, his expression venomous. "You owe me. Refuse to pay and you will suffer. I am not a man you want as your enemy."

"You can't stay here. This is my place of work. Go. I'll ring you. Arrange something for later."

"Shaw is dead. He was my contact. The kid who shot him is also dead. I am a man of little patience." Todoran grabbed Horton by the lapels of his suit jacket. "I repeat — I need that money now!"

Horton was shaking with terror. He felt the villain reach into the inside pocket of his suit jacket and remove his wallet. He watched as Todoran flicked through the contents, finally removing several notes.

"This is peanuts. I am owed thousands. Get my money from your boss. Fail to do that and I will be back. I will not waste time talking. I will simply shoot you dead!"

The Romanian slipped out of the rear entrance and drove away. Horton watched until he was out of sight. The man was a very real threat. He had meant every word. Everything was spiralling out of control. Time to wind the operation up.

Horton was walking towards his office when he heard the sirens. A number of police cars, followed by DCI Greco, were speeding into the car park. For one brief moment Horton considered running, then he changed his mind. If he did that, he'd be on his own.

Greco stalked into the clinic, waving a document at Horton. "We have a warrant. We will go through this place brick by brick if we have to."

"Tell me what you're looking for. Perhaps I can help." Horton was as smooth as ever.

"A boy called Farid had his kidney removed here, illegally. He is a minor, smuggled into this country from Calais."

Horton looked unruffled. "Nonsense. Who has been feeding you this rubbish?"

"The boy himself told us. We have also cleared the factory in Openshaw this morning. I'll be interested to hear what Mr Hussain has to say for himself."

Horton's face was murderous. He was about to respond when Faisal Rashid appeared.

"Tell them, Jason. Whatever you have been doing, just admit it."

Horton turned on his partner. "Shut up, Faisal. You know nothing!"

"I know you owed that low-life Shaw a small fortune! What did he demand as payment, Jason?"

Greco looked at the doctor. "Is that true? Were you aware of what your partner was up to?"

"I had an inkling. I was suspicious when Hamid Khan told me that Jason had promised him a new kidney. I knew there was no family donor."

"Didn't you say anything?" Greco asked.

He shook his head. "No, I was weak. I knew Jason was in financial trouble with that man, Shaw. It was affecting the clinic. I just wanted things put right. I did not want any trouble for the clinic."

"Well, you're going to get a shedload of trouble now," Grace assured him. "We don't think the boy we're looking after was the only one."

Faisal Rashid looked terrified.

"Tell us what you know, Doctor Rashid."

"I have seen things, heard things, usually late at night. Boys brought here. The theatres being used. Outside staff being called in when we've plenty of our own."

"And you turned a blind eye." Greco could barely believe what he was hearing. He turned to Horton.

"How many? How many young men have you butchered in this way?"

"Surgery, please, not butchery." Horton seemed almost proud of what he'd done. "There have been more than I can remember. I owed Shaw, which is not advisable. The man was an animal. It is a lucrative trade, and I could easily pay him off that way. We supply other private hospitals, in this country but more often abroad. A healthy kidney is worth its weight in gold."

"You keep records?"

"Of course. Each boy signs a consent form."

Greco shook his head. *More than I can remember . . .* "They are in the country illegally and under age. Your forms will not stand up, Doctor Horton. Who brought the boys in?"

"That was Shaw's job. He had the contacts, the drivers. He arranged to supply the factories, restaurants and any other business that required cheap labour. Not only in Manchester, but across the country."

"On his own?" Greco doubted this. From what he'd read and understood, Shaw had been very much a local villain, Vinny Costello's man in this area. If Vinny was no longer up to it, then Horton would know who had the real power.

"There may have been an organisation behind Shaw, I don't know. We never talked about it."

He was lying. Horton knew very well who was behind it. "I think you do. We know that Vinny Costello is ill. There have been changes. Who runs things now?"

"I'm a surgeon, not a hoodlum. I leave such details to others."

More lies. "How did the operation work?"

"It was beautifully simple. The boys are brought to me. I run tests. If the boys are suitable, they are brought here later for surgery. In the main they are none the worse for it. A few weeks' recuperation and they are as good as new. The benefit to others in need is immeasurable. People are given a second chance at life." He paused. "I don't regret what I've done. I made money, yes, but that was not the prime motive. I'm a doctor. I am here to save lives."

A uniformed officer was fastening the cuffs.

Grace nudged Greco. "He's bloody mad!" she whispered. "He thinks he can rationalise it away. Wait until he comes up against a jury!"

"Were you involved in bringing the boys into the country?"

"No, that was down to others."

"Who, Doctor Horton?"

"Like I've already told you, I never knew the details." He smiled.

Horton and Rashid were both taken away. Greco believed that Rashid hadn't take part in it, but he had admitted that he suspected what was happening. It was up to the CPS now.

They watched them leave, and Grace turned to Greco. "So, apart from the surgery, what part did Horton play in it all? Did he order the boys killed when they escaped? Or was that Shaw taking matters into his own hands? And where does Todoran fit in? I can see how Horton would need someone like him, but to go out there and find him," she shook her head, "He doesn't move in those circles."

"But he does," Greco reminded her. "Sadie Costello — remember?"

Chapter 26

Once the operation at the factory was over, Leah dropped Speedy back at the station and made for the Grapes pub. She needed to know what Rouse wanted from Roman.

She was in no mood to play games. She'd had a quick phone conversation with Greco which made her think. The DCI didn't think Horton was behind bringing the lads into the country. Neither did he think Horton had given the order to kill Jamal and the other young man. So who had? Now that Horton and Rashid were under lock and key, there was no one left. No one that they knew about.

Leah strode into the Grapes. Ignoring the whistles and comments, she sat down by the window. Within minutes, Roman appeared from an adjoining room.

He smiled at her. "Back again, doll. What is it now?"

"Tony Rouse came to see you. Why? What did he want?"

He sat down beside her. "My conversations with the other people I feed information to are confidential. If I tell you, and you act on it, Rouse will know it was me."

"Cut the crap, Roman. We are close to the end of this now, but there are still bits of the puzzle missing. We know about the boys, and the slave labour. Immigration are on the job and they will put a stop to it. We know about the doctor and what he was up to." She looked straight at him. "But that's not enough. We have to find out who is at the back of this."

He gave her a big smile. "The good doctor. Stands to reason. He had the most to gain."

"He is interested in making money and saving lives. Greco thinks he's close to losing his mind. So no, Roman, it isn't him. He doesn't have the clout."

"In that case, you have a problem, doll. Have you considered Slicer for the role of top dog?"

"He's dead, as well you know." She paused. "Costello — what's he up to?"

"Vinny is ill," Roman reminded her.

"Seriously ill is what we've heard. But what exactly is his problem?"

Roman seemed reluctant to say. "It's not common knowledge, for obvious reasons. Folk find out that Vinny's not up to it and we'll have an all-out war. There are plenty of villains out there, eager to snatch the crown. He had a heart attack a few weeks ago. The hospital attempted bypass surgery but when they got in there, the attack had done too much damage — valves and the like. At his age, the best option was to stitch him back together and do nothing."

"So his time is limited?"

"Very much so."

"Who will he hand over to?"

Roman took a swig of his beer. He made out he was thinking about it, but Leah was sure he knew more than he was saying.

"The changeover has already happened, weeks ago. New people are gradually being put in place. Things are set to be run very different. When the time is right, others will be told."

"This new boss — tough, is he?"

"Runs things with an iron fist. Hired new people, operating scams that would shame the devil."

The words hung in the air between them. Leah was thinking hard, trying to make sense of what Roman had just said.

"You could have told me this in the first place, Roman. It would have saved us a lot of trouble."

"I have to be careful. A matter of survival," he reminded her.

Leah could only imagine the fine line Roman walked. The villains trusted him for now. But if they ever got the slightest inkling that he'd double-crossed them . . .

"Rouse found out about the changeover?"

"He guessed. The fool started to blab. Vinny didn't like it, neither did the new boss."

"So Costello is fine with the new setup. He's happy for someone new to take over?"

"Not happy, but he has no choice. All these years of being top dog, and now he is forced to hand over power to another. But that doesn't stop him having input. He wants a gradual handing over. He does not want all-out war on the streets as every scally that's ever fancied his chances has a go."

"Who is it, Roman?" she asked firmly. "His opener was the smuggling of vulnerable young men from the Calais camp. We can't let him get away with it."

Roman smiled again. "Do you have proof? I doubt it. This one is careful. Never gets dirty hands. Learned off the master."

"So you won't help?"

"You need to think harder, doll. Like I said, Rouse worked it out, and he's not that bright. That's what got him into so much trouble. He found out about the lads and that clinic, but he didn't stop digging. Nearly dug himself into an early grave. The power might be vested in a different pair of hands, but that is not for general consumption — not yet anyway."

"Stop arsing me about, Roman. I need a name."

"You've heard the one about the apple not falling far from the tree?"

* * *

"Sadie Costello!" Grace repeated. "She is behind all this?"

"According to my informant — not that he admitted it in so many words," Leah replied. "But he gave me a damn good clue, and I have no reason to doubt him. If you think about it, she is in the perfect position to take over from her father. Vinny is ill, but to maintain order he wanted this kept quiet until he'd spoken to certain key people. Slicer Shaw for one. God knows who else. Rouse found out. Got too close to the whole operation — the boys, the killings and the sale of organs. Which is why they wanted him dead."

"Do we know where Rouse is now?" asked Greco.

"Roman reckons he'll lay low for a while longer. Eventually news of Costello's fall from power will be common knowledge, and he'll be able to show his face again."

"Did Rouse have any evidence on Sadie?"

"No. He worked it out, but said things to the wrong people. Slicer Shaw, for one."

Greco was angry. "I want everything we have going over again. All the statements, all the CCTV footage. We need something, anything that will incriminate Sadie Costello."

Leah shook her head. "Bet we don't find anything. She is like her father — gets others to dirty their hands."

"Horton must know. He and Sadie were close. I wonder if he will talk to us?" Greco said.

"If he does, then he's dead. Even behind bars he'll not be safe. He must know this, he's not daft. So I doubt it." Leah was firm.

"No chance of her trying to get him off?"

"I don't think so, sir. All that affection at the club was probably a performance. All Sadie was really interested in was his skill as a surgeon."

"Todoran?"

Joel Hough spoke up. "We have had the results back, sir. The blood found by the doors was a match. That puts him at the scene. The blood and tissue on the hammer did belong to Dent. The blade found on Dent had DNA that matches the two dead boys. And still no sign of Dent's mobile phone."

That resolved the murder of Jamal and the unknown boy. "In that case, we need to find Todoran. We've alerted the ports? Dover especially."

Joel nodded. "We've had an update on his vehicle, sir. Todoran's lorry was found abandoned at a service station on the M20. A number of refugees were hidden on board."

"Any clue where Todoran might have gone?"

"Not yet, sir."

Greco walked over to the incident board. The team sat at their desks completing their reports. It wasn't the outcome he'd wanted. Granted they had Horton. But now that he knew about the bigger picture, he wanted Sadie Costello behind bars. He stared at the board. How likely was that? There was nothing there that would help. She may have orchestrated the operation, but unless Horton talked, they didn't have a scrap of evidence against her.

Epilogue

6 weeks later

"Stephen!" It was Superintendent Gordon McCabe, shouting down the corridor.

"Immigration have finally finished processing those lads from the factory your people raided. Very few spoke English so it was a thankless task, and no help with regard to the case. Hussain reckons he dealt only with Ray Shaw. Maintains he's no idea who was behind the operation." He shook his head. "God knows how many more such places there are on our patch. But at least it'll be a hefty prison sentence for Hussain."

"Todoran was picked up in France yesterday," Greco told him. "They found a number of mobile phones on him, one of them belonging to Michael Dent. It seems it was Dent that sent Rouse the message. He must have found his number in Crompton's notebook. Todoran is willing to do a deal. He knows nothing about the organisation of the operation. He only ever spoke to Shaw, and once to Horton. But he is willing to tell us who his friends are at Border Control. The ones who, for a fee, turn a blind eye."

McCabe shrugged. "It can't be much of a deal. He's going down for killing Dent. And the big one? Sadie Costello?"

"Nothing, sir. Horton refuses to say anything against her. A major disappointment."

Greco carried on towards the incident room, where Leah had just put the phone down.

"The case against Horton is sound. He'll go down for a good few years. There's not enough to charge Rashid, though. He might have known stuff but there is no evidence to prove it. Horton certainly hasn't dropped him in it. He still maintains Sadie knew nothing."

"He's lying. But Sadie Costello isn't going away, and neither is the rest of the operation. We took out only a small part of what is going on nationwide. We have to hope that she drops her guard in the future," Greco said.

"Not good though, is it, sir?" Speedy piped up. "Bloody irritating, if you ask me. A scam like that, and she walks."

Greco smiled at his sergeant. "At least we have put a stop to it on our patch."

* * *

"Can I have a word?" Grace had arrived late that morning and had said little. "We can get a coffee from the canteen."

What now? Grace's 'private words' always bugged Greco. The Brighton incident hadn't been forgotten but she'd not been on about it as much lately. He was hopeful that in time she would let it drop. That way he wouldn't have to make a decision about her one way or the other.

"I'll get them. You sit over there." She nodded to a table at the far end of the room.

Greco checked his phone while he waited. It was the half-term holidays and Pat had taken Matilda to see Suzy's parents in Norfolk. She was sending him regular updates and photos. Looking through them, he could see that his daughter was having a great time.

Grace put down his coffee.

"Orange juice? Not like you."

Grace shook her head. "Gone off coffee. And tea."

"Health kick?"

"No, Stephen, it's nothing that simple."

There was something about her tone, edgy, uncomfortable. He met her gaze for an instant. She looked down.

"There is never going to be a right time to say this, so I'll just come out with it." Grace took a deep breath.

"I'm pregnant, Stephen — with your child."

THE END

Thank you for reading this book. If you enjoyed it please leave feedback on Amazon, and if there is anything we missed or you have a question about then please get in touch. The author and publishing team appreciate your feedback and time reading this book.

Our email is office@joffebooks.com

www.joffebooks.com

ALSO BY HELEN H. DURRANT

CALLADINE & BAYLISS MYSTERIES
DEAD WRONG
DEAD SILENT
DEAD LIST
DEAD LOST
DEAD & BURIED
DEAD NASTY

DI GRECO
DARK MURDER
DARK HOUSES
DARK TRADE

21057008R00125

Printed in Great Britain
by Amazon